FLOOD:
Race Against Time

All inquiries should be addressed to:
Barron's Educational Series, Inc.
250 Wireless Boulevard
Hauppauge, New York 11788
www.barronseduc.com

ISBN: 978-1-4380-0805-9

Library of Congress Control Number: 2016022575

Date of Manufacture: August 2016
Manufactured by: B12V12G

Printed in the United States of America

9 8 7 6 5 4 3 2 1

S.T.E.M.

SQUAD

FLOOD:

Race Against Time

Aaron Rosenberg
Illustrated by Deb Gross

BARRON'S

S.T.E.M.

SQUAD

Julie Robbins

Malik Jamar

Christopher Wong

Tracey DeGuerra

Ilyana Desoff

CHAPTER 1

A WET START

"Man, this rain is crazy!" Malik Jamar complained as he dashed from the car. It was barely eight o'clock in the morning, but already it was pouring so hard that the water was coming down less in droplets than in torrents, as if someone had dumped an ocean on their heads. Clutching his umbrella, its canopy brushing his hair and hanging so low that he couldn't see above waist level, Malik slammed the door shut behind him and ran down the sidewalk toward the school's front door. The wind was strong enough that he had to hold on tight to keep the umbrella from getting blown away, and the rain was gusting almost sideways, making the cover mostly useless anyway.

Other students were also bolting for shelter—and was that a really small, really hairy guy in a bright yellow raincoat zooming past him on a bike? Between the wind and the rain, Malik couldn't be sure, and when he blinked the water out of his eyes, the strange figure was gone.

What a way to start the new school year!

Once he was inside, however, Malik felt better. He'd thought to wear galoshes, so his feet were still dry. The umbrella had kept his head mostly covered, and the transparent rain slicker he'd worn had covered his shirt and his jeans down to the knees. He'd gotten a little wet below that, but compared to the other kids, he wasn't nearly as soaked. He smirked as he finished surveying the damage. Still looking good!

Admittedly, he wasn't feeling his best. There was a pressure behind his eyes, like a headache that wasn't quite there yet but was threatening to show up, and his nose was plugged up too. Malik had worried that he might be coming down with something, but his father had set him straight. "It's the barometric pressure," he'd explained as they had headed to school. "All this rain and those heavy storm clouds mean there's a lot of pressure in the air, and you're feeling it in your head. When the storm finally passes, that headache'll

Barometric pressure is another name for atmospheric pressure, or the pressure that the air exerts on a given area. The term comes from the fact that a barometer is a tool used to measure air pressure. Air has weight and density, and it's a combination of those factors, plus the air's temperature and its height above the Earth's surface, that determines its pressure. Air pressure is most often measured in hectopascals (or millibars). Weather systems can drastically change the air pressure, and the sudden change often affects people, particularly in the ears and nose and in the joints.

disappear." Malik couldn't wait. He was glad he hadn't had to miss the first day of school, though—what an impression that would have made!

Holding the umbrella out well in front of him so it wouldn't drip on him, Malik navigated the crowded halls toward his locker. His parents had brought him to Albert Einstein Magnet High School ("Go Magnets!") a few weeks back for orientation, and he'd taken the time since then to memorize the map they'd provided, among other things. That was just the way he'd always been—he liked knowing where he was, how to get there, and what was around him.

Along the way he stopped to say hello to some other kids he knew from his old school. "Yo, Malik!" one of the girls, Cassie, called out as he passed. "Looking sharp!" Cassie was Lebanese, like him, and their families had been friends their whole lives. Cassie was cool—Malik would have been friends with her anyway.

"You too, Cassie," he replied with a wave, but didn't slow down. "Got to get rid of the rain gear," he explained over his shoulder. "Later!"

Cassie's gotten taller, he thought as he moved away. And that new haircut looks good on her. He'd have to tell her that if he ran into her again later. It was the little things, and Malik prided himself on noticing details.

Reaching his locker, he spun the combination with practiced ease. "Man, how'd you do that?" another kid a few spaces over asked, staring as Malik's locker opened on the first try. "I've been working on mine for ten minutes!"

"You've got to start out at zero," Malik explained, transferring the umbrella to a plastic bag he'd pulled from his backpack and then hanging that on one of the hooks inside. "Spin left to the first number, then go right and all the way past the first number to the next, then back left again without circling all the way around. Then push it in a little. Should do the trick." He shrugged nonchalantly, pretending he hadn't practiced at home on a similar-style lock for a half hour to make sure he could get it right, as he removed the slicker and then bent to get his galoshes. He quickly put on his shoes so he wasn't standing there in his socks too long.

"Oh, okay. Thanks!" His new neighbor tried that, squinting in concentration, and then grinned when it worked. "Sweet!" He turned back to Malik. "Hey, I'm Sam. Sam Quick."

"Malik Jamar," Malik replied. He eased his locker shut again. No books yet, so it was empty except for the rain gear—and the mirror he'd stuck on the inside of the door when they'd gone to find it during orientation. He'd already checked his hair in the reflection and confirmed that it still looked good. Score!

He'd also studied Sam, evaluating him quickly. Decent height, big but not heavy, probably into sports. Clothes were basic—jeans and a red T-shirt with an abstract image of a basketball player, definitely not designer but not terrible, and colors that worked with Sam's dark hair. He had basketball shoes like Malik did, but they were a little scuffed and definitely worn in. Clearly a jock, Malik decided.

"Nice kicks," he offered. "Air Jordans, am I right?"

"Oh, yeah." Sam smiled again. "Thanks! Yours are sick, too." A loud thunderclap shook overhead, making them both jump. "This rain is nuts, right?" Sam asked. "I heard on the radio that the rainfall today is already higher than the last two weeks combined."

"Nuts," Malik agreed. He'd heard the same meteorologist's report and still remembered the statistics—ten to twelve inches expected today, the highest rainfall on this date in seventeen years, plus a 95 percent chance of rain tomorrow and a 70 percent chance the day after that. He'd always been good at remembering facts.

Another sound echoed through the halls, but this time it was the clang of a bell. "Right, got to get to class," Sam said. "Catch you later. And thanks!"

"Yeah, no worries," Malik replied, hoisting his bag onto his shoulder and turning to head toward his own first class.

He had a feeling he was really going to like it here.

The rest of the day went well. Malik was polite and on time, so he made a good impression on each of his teachers. Plus, he was always prepared to take notes, while a lot of his classmates were still gazing around and chatting with one another. Malik was happy to talk to people between classes, but once the teacher cleared his or her throat, he was eyes front and all attention. You didn't want to get labeled a troublemaker, especially on the first day!

Lunch was crazy, of course. Einstein was as big as his old school, maybe bigger, and there was only one lunch per grade, so all of the ninth graders crowded into the cafeteria together. The room was big enough for all of them, of course—it had been renovated over the summer and was clean and modern now, with big windows all along two sides and gleaming new floors and sturdy tables with attached benches arranged in rows. Teachers were available to help, directing kids where to go. It was just a madhouse getting everyone in there.

Malik glanced at the windows. It was still coming down hard outside, the deluge beating against the windows in a steady beat. Southern California was used to the occasional rainstorm, but this was something else. Malik wasn't sure he'd ever seen it rain this hard before. He hoped it'd let up soon. Carrying the umbrella and slicker every day would be a chore, especially now that his backpack was filled with new textbooks and workbooks.

A lot of kids were milling about, looking for classmates they knew and trying to figure out where to sit, but once he had his food, Malik didn't hesitate. He'd spotted Cassie sitting at a table in the back right corner, so he made a beeline for her.

As he headed confidently toward the table, a woman's voice stopped Malik in his tracks. "I don't know how I let you talk me into this," she said.

At first, Malik thought she was talking to him, even though he didn't see her anywhere or recognize the voice and had no idea what she was talking about. But then a man replied. Or at least Malik thought it was a reply!

"It'll be fine," the man said. "Trust me."

"Is it even safe?" she asked.

"Safe? Of course it is! It's only STEM, after all. This isn't like that time in Istanbul—although I will say, those scarves held out a lot longer than I'd expected . . ."

Malik realized he was standing completely still, lunch tray in hand, shamelessly eavesdropping. He quickly gathered himself and headed for Cassie's table. Whatever those two were talking about, it had nothing to do with him! Besides, they were adults here, which meant they were teachers, security guards, or staff. And all three of those were people he had to trust to do their jobs right—and people who could make his life difficult if they thought he'd been snooping on their private conversation.

He pushed all thoughts of the strange discussion aside as he joined Cassie. A few other friends from his old school were already seated and eating, and everyone called out hellos as Malik sat down. He grinned as he returned the greetings. First day, and he already felt comfortable in his new school.

He definitely planned to keep it that way.

Everything was going exactly according to plan— until science class.

"Welcome to eighth-grade science," their teacher, Mrs. Cavanaugh, announced once everyone was seated. "Please clear your desks except for a pencil."

And she started walking up and down the rows, handing stapled packets to each student.

At first Malik thought this was just a handout, maybe the class outline, but then he heard the protests from the kids in front of him. "A test?" one girl complained as she grudgingly took the pages. "It's the first day!"

"This isn't part of your grade," Mrs. Cavanaugh reassured them, finishing her circuit of the room and returning to her desk. "It's more of an evaluation to see where each of you stands in terms of what you already know. But please do complete it to the best of your ability. That way we can make sure you're getting the education that works best for you."

Malik studied the papers in front of him and sighed. Great. He was usually fine with tests—it was just a matter of putting the right information in the right place, and organization was something he was good at—but science? Science wasn't exactly his favorite subject.

Well, there wasn't much he could do about it. He picked up his pencil and started reading.

The test was strange. It was a mix of questions, and Malik couldn't see any sense to how they were ordered. There'd be a math problem, and then after it would be a question about how to handle downloads on your phone. Next would be a chemical formula you had to balance, and then a question about the best place to stand during an earthquake. It was weird. He did the best he could, both because those were the instructions and because he couldn't see not trying his hardest. That was just the way he'd been raised. Some of the questions were easy, some were hard, some he had absolutely no idea how to answer, and a few—like the formulae and some of the word problems—were actually fun. He finished just before the bell rang and handed his test in with everyone else. Whew!

"We'll go over the class outline tomorrow," Mrs. Cavanaugh called out as kids grabbed their bags and rushed out to find their next class. "Read the first chapter in your textbook, the overview. Bye!"

Swell—first a test, and now homework. On the first day! At least it was just an overview, Malik thought as he joined the line out the door and then headed to English. Basically a long introduction. He could handle that.

The next day didn't start out as well. First of all, it was still pouring. "I could take the bus, you know," Malik told his dad as he drove slowly and carefully, leaning forward to see past the windshield wipers whipping around frantically in their attempts to keep the front window clear. Malik kept his eyes open for that same weird bicyclist from the day before but didn't see him. Or her. Or it.

"Sure, sure," his father agreed, not taking his eyes off the road or both hands off the wheel. "Maybe next week. But this is your first week there. Want to make sure you start off each day on the right foot." He swerved to avoid a massive puddle. "That was close!"

Malik bit back a laugh. He loved his dad, and it was really kind of him to take time out of his own busy schedule to drive Malik each morning. But he wasn't the best driver in perfect weather, and this rain was insane! Still, he knew mentioning that would only hurt his dad's feelings, so he kept his mouth shut. It was only one week, after all. And surely the rain would stop soon!

A few minutes later, Malik's dad actually had good reason to be concerned. They were approaching a major intersection, and the entire thing was under water! Malik's dad slowed down, clearly not sure how to proceed. Other cars were forcing their way across, so he gritted his teeth and decided to go for it.

Those other cars were much bigger than their little sedan, however. And when they hit the middle of the intersection, where the water was deepest, and started sliding sideways, Malik's dad realized he'd made the wrong decision!

"Hold on!" he shouted, twisting the steering wheel wildly in an attempt to get control again. But that only seemed to make things worse. The car started spinning itself, but in the wrong direction, toward the cross street rather than straight ahead, where they needed to go. And they were still drifting!

"Punch it, Dad!" Malik yelled, and for once his father didn't argue. He floored the gas pedal, and the little car's engine roared. They could hear the wheels spinning like crazy, but there was nothing for them to catch on. They were at the water's mercy!

It was the curb that saved them. The water had carried them sideways a bit, and the front passenger tire bumped up against the corner curb. The wheel found some purchase there, and there was a jolt as the car lurched forward. Then the back wheel also caught hold, and suddenly they were moving under their own power again! Malik's dad still had the gas pedal to the floor, and the car practically growled as it launched itself forward and across the street, right through the water. Their forward momentum overcame the current, and a long, tense minute later their tires had gripped the road on the other side and they were zooming off the curb and back onto the street past the flooded area.

"Wow!" Malik exclaimed. "Way to go, Dad!"

His father managed a weak smile in return. "I think I'll invest in some better tires after I drop you off," he said shakily. "Or maybe just a boat."

Malik laughed, but he knew his dad was really worried. So was he. If it was this bad now, what would the roads be like if this rain continued?

12

The rest of the way to school was uneventful, and Malik managed to slip into homeroom just before the late bell sounded. But when the teacher got to his name, she frowned. Then she flipped up the attendance sheet to read something else beneath it.

"Malik, you're to go to the main office," she told him. "Right away."

"Uh, okay." Malik gathered his things and rose from his chair. "Is something wrong?"

His teacher just shook her head and shooed him toward the door. "All it says is for you to head to the office. Hurry, or you'll be late for your first class."

Malik hurried. And worried. What did the office want with him? He'd never been a troublemaker, and it was only the second day, anyway!

Reaching the main office, Malik stepped up to the front desk and gave the secretary his name. "Oh, yes," she said, peering around her desk for a second. "Where did I put that? Here it is!" She grabbed a sheet off a small stack, glanced at it quickly, then handed it to him. "Schedule change, sweetie. Your last two periods got swapped."

"Really?" Malik studied the sheet. Sure enough, he now had English sixth period and Science seventh— except instead of saying "8th-Gr. Scnce" like it had before, now his science class was listed as "STEM1." STEM, he thought. Like that conversation he'd overheard at lunch yesterday! The one where the woman asked if it was dangerous!

"What's STEM?" he asked the secretary, showing her where it was printed.

"Oh, that's Mr. Enright's class." She flushed a little, and actually giggled. "You'll like him. He's a doll!" Just then the bell marking the end of homeroom sounded. "Oh, you'd better hurry along, dear," the secretary told Malik. "Have a good day!"

"Yeah, thanks, you too," Malik replied automatically, turning and leaving the office. At least the rest of his classes were the same! He didn't mind switching English too much—he'd only known one other kid in the class yesterday, and though everyone else had seemed nice enough, it wasn't a big deal for him to switch. He was a little worried about this new science class, though.

Still, it wasn't like he could do anything about it now. He'd just have to hope for the best. At least this Mr. Enright was "a doll," Malik thought with a laugh as he headed down the hall. That's sure to help!

After English that day—it was with the same teacher, and Malik knew a few other kids in his class, so that was a bonus—Malik pulled out his new schedule to see where he was going next. He'd memorized the routes for his classes before school had started, of course, but that had been for the old schedule, not this new one. When he saw what it said, though, he frowned.

Room 103B? "One-oh-three-B?" he said aloud. "Where's that?" He thought he knew where 103 was, though he didn't have any classes over that way, but he didn't remember seeing a 103B on the map!

His English teacher, Mr. Donalty, overheard him. "That's at the end of the left corridor," he answered. "I thought that was still under construction, actually. I guess they finished early." With a shrug, Mr. Donalty pointed toward the clock. "You'd better hurry. Don't want to be late."

"Right. Thank you." With a sigh, Malik headed for the door. They were midway down the right corridor, so he'd have to return to the central hall and then go all the way down the building's left side. And he was right; he'd have to hurry. He hated being late, at least in school, where the teachers wanted you there on time or early. Social events were different—being a little late was the way to go so that you could make sure you weren't the first one there.

As he left the room, Malik thought he caught a flash of movement at the end of the corridor. But it was too small and too dark to be another student. Was there a dog running loose in here? That seemed unlikely, and he didn't really have time to worry about it.

Walking as quickly as he dared, Malik dashed down the hall. But just as he burst out into the main hall, someone appeared in front him, also moving fast. There was no time to slow down or swerve, and Malik ran right into the person. They collided hard enough that he was knocked right off his feet, landing awkwardly on his backpack.

"Hey!" he shouted, glaring at whoever it was as he twisted around, trying to stand back up. "Watch where you're going!"

Then he saw who it was and groaned.

Oh, great! Just what he needed!

CHAPTER 2

COLLISION COURSE

Julie "Jules" Robbins frowned down at Malik, who was on the ground in front of her, and sighed. Why did it have to be him?

For the most part, the first two days of high school had gone well. Her teachers all seemed okay, she'd run into a few friends from middle school, she'd made a few new potential friends, and Coach had been really impressed with her in PE and had practically cried when Jules had said that she'd been planning to try out for the basketball team after school.

About the only sour note was running into Malik Jamar.

He wasn't a mean kid or anything like that. He wasn't even a bully. But something about him just rubbed her the wrong way. Maybe it was the way everything about him always had to be just so—his hair done perfectly, his clothes carefully picked out and precisely arranged, all of his gear the latest and coolest. He was a like a male model, or maybe a store dummy, all decked out and dolled up and perfect on the outside but completely stiff, with nothing showing underneath. Was there even a real person in there? Or maybe it was the fact that he got along with absolutely everyone. Nobody did that—there were always people you liked and others you didn't, and there were always people who didn't like you too. But not Malik. He got along with everyone—except her, it seemed. That just struck Jules as fake somehow. And she didn't have the time or the energy to deal with fake.

So of course he had to literally run into her. Or they had to run into each other.

Apparently she wasn't going to be able to avoid him as easily here as she had at their old school.

They stared at each other for a few seconds more before Malik slowly levered himself back to his feet. "Nothing broken, thanks for asking," he told her, brushing himself off. "And for offering me a hand up."

"Look where you're going next time," Jules advised gruffly. She turned away, taking a few steps the way she'd been heading before all this. She didn't have time for Malik's melodrama.

"Yeah, well, that's not my fault," he replied, starting in the same direction. Was he following her? "I was trying not to be late for class." There was a clock mounted on the wall of the main hall, and he frowned at it. Jules glanced over there as well and quickly increased her pace. She actually would be late if she didn't hurry!

Walking as quickly as she dared, she sped down the corridor. She scanned room numbers as she went. 106 . . . 105 . . . 104 . . . 103.

But where was 103B?

"You've got to be kidding me," Malik muttered behind her. Jules turned to glare at him.

"What do you want?" she demanded.

Malik actually stared at her like she was making no sense. "I'm just looking for this screwy class," he answered finally. "What do *you* want?"

"The same." Jules was getting a sinking feeling in her stomach. That only intensified when Malik held up the slip of paper in his hand. It was a class schedule, and the last class was listed as "STEM1."

Same as the last class on the revised schedule she was holding herself.

Great.

"We're in the same class?" Malik asked softly, staring at the two papers. "Swell." Then he seemed to realize she was still there and plastered an obviously fake—even for him—smile across his face. "I mean, that's great!" He turned his full attention to the paper instead. "But this says it's 103B. I don't see a 'B,' do you?"

As much as Jules wished she could just walk away

and leave Malik there, she studied her own paper and the doorframes lining the hall. "No," she admitted. "But this is 103; maybe they'll know."

And she pushed the door open.

"Ask for help like some newbie—great, awesome plan," Malik muttered at her back. But he followed her into the classroom.

It was smaller—and dingier—than most of the other rooms she'd been in today. Hadn't she heard something about them renovating the school? Had they just not gotten to this part yet? It certainly looked like it hadn't been touched in years. The chairs were old and chipped, the desks were covered in writing and doodles from years of use, and the floor had been worn down to the point that it was slick as though wet and was uneven in places. It was like being in the school version of an old ghost town.

Nor was there any sign of a teacher. The chalkboard, old and almost gray from use, was nonetheless blank beyond the faint marks left from previous classes.

The only other people there were the three students who had all turned to stare when Jules and then Malik had entered the room.

"Yo," one of the two girls, a broad-shouldered Hispanic girl with close-cropped hair, called out. "You guys here for STEM1?"

"Right," Jules confirmed. "Where is everybody?"

"No idea," the other girl, a petite thing with long, snow-white blond hair, said. "It's like one of those alien abduction movies; they took everyone but the five of us." She offered a shy smile. "I'm Ilyana, by the way."

"Jules," she replied. She was already studying the room. There were no signs of textbooks or lab supplies or anything. It was just old chairs, old desks, an equally old teacher desk, and them. What was going on here?

Malik introduced himself to the two girls as well, and to the third kid, a tall, skinny Asian boy decked out in a black leather jacket, black band T-shirt, and jeans. "I really hope we don't get docked for being late," the boy, whose name was Christopher, complained. "We did exactly what we were supposed to do!" He glanced anxiously at his watch. "This isn't a very fair way to start out the year."

"I'm sure it's just a little glitch," Malik said. "They'll figure out the mistake soon, and then we can go find our real classroom." Jules knew he was trying to help, but it still felt like he was saying what he thought people wanted to hear, rather than what he really thought.

"Whatever." The first girl, Tracey, leaned against the sturdy wooden teacher desk, arms folded across her chest. "I'm not exactly in a hurry to start class."

Christopher harrumphed and moved toward the door, most likely to keep watch for their missing teacher. Ilyana just sighed, sank into a chair, and pulled a tablet from her bag. She immediately disappeared behind its small screen. By the way her eyes were moving left to right and then back again, Jules suspected the other girl was reading.

Jules shook her head. Great. Five kids, all in what might or might not be the right classroom, with no sign of the teacher. And three of those kids were occupying themselves.

Which meant if she wanted to talk to anyone . . . it would have to be Malik.

She just wasn't sure she was desperate enough for that.

Yet.

It was a huge relief when the door to the hall opened again and a sixth person entered the room.

CHAPTER 3

BOILING POINT

"Hello there!" The man was tall and skinny, with slightly long, slightly wavy black hair and a long nose. He was carrying a clipboard—and wearing a full black tuxedo! "Sorry I'm a little late. I had to stop and clear up a few things with the principal. I'm Mr. Enright, your teacher."

"So this is the right room for STEM1?" Christopher asked, tailing after their new teacher. "We weren't sure—the transfer notice said 103B." He looked a little more relaxed now that he knew he wouldn't be marked as tardy.

"Oh, yes, sorry about that," Mr. Enright chuckled. He had a British accent, Jules noticed. It was kind of cool. "That's just a little joke on my part. This is where we'll meet each day, but it's not our classroom. Not really."

And without saying anything else, he turned and walked right through the chalkboard, disappearing completely from sight as if the classroom fixture had swallowed him whole.

"What the heck?" Jules blurted out. Behind her, the other kids all gasped as well.

"A hologram!" Ilyana whispered, her whole face lit up. "Just like on *Star Trek*! That's awesome!" And, hopping off the desk, she grabbed her bag and hurried after their now-vanished teacher. She disappeared as well.

A **hologram** is a three-dimensional image, meaning an image that has depth to it, that can be seen without the use of special glasses or other equipment. Most holograms are projected images rather than images printed onto a two-dimensional shape.

"Come on, you guys!" her voice wafted back a second later. "This is so amazing! It's like jumping onto Platform 9 3/4!"

Christopher was next, with Malik right behind him. Tracey glanced at Jules and shrugged, then joined the odd little procession. With a sigh, Jules brought up the rear.

She couldn't help herself from tensing up right before her foot hit the wall, but it passed through easily, and the rest of her followed immediately after. She saw an odd blur or flicker of color as her head cleared, but then she was through.

And gasped at the sight before her.

The dingy old classroom was gone. Instead, she was staring at a gleaming metallic wall, all shiny and new. The floor was new as well—a deep rich blue in color and patterned with dollar-sized circles—and it had a springy feel like rubber, squeaking slightly beneath her shoes. The lighting was hidden along a narrow ledge just below the ceiling, so that the area was lit in a soft, even glow, and Jules could hear the faint hum of machinery.

On a whim, she glanced back over her shoulder. Room 103 was clearly visible there, though it looked like a thin, gauzy curtain had been drawn across it.

". . . not actually a hologram," Mr. Enright was explaining to Ilyana, who listened intently. "It's an array of high-definition digital projectors set all around the edge and projecting a collective image of the wall." He chuckled again—he seemed like the kind of teacher who laughed a lot, and not just at students. "Wouldn't want just anyone stumbling in here!"

Glancing around, the teacher spotted Jules and nodded. "Right, everyone is present and accounted for. Let's go." He pressed a large button on the wall behind him, and with a faint hiss and a muted hum the wall parted, revealing a large, brightly lit metal box.

An elevator.

The school had an elevator? Off an old classroom? Hidden behind a fake wall?

What was this class, anyway?

But Mr. Enright didn't hesitate, leading them into the elevator car, and Jules followed along with the rest. There were only two buttons, marked "S" and "C," above the usual Door Close, Door Open, and Emergency Call ones, and once everyone was inside, Mr. Enright said from the back, "Would someone kindly hit C, please?"

"I've got it!" Christopher answered quickly, even though he had to squirm past Jules and Tracey to manage. It was already obvious that despite his punk-rock appearance, he was the kind of kid who would do anything to keep his teachers happy. Jules rolled her eyes a little and almost laughed when she saw Tracey do the same. They smirked at each other as the elevator doors slid shut and the car began its descent.

It was smooth and quiet, but it felt fast too. "How far down are we going?" Jules asked. She'd assumed they had to be going down, since the school was only one story tall, but then again she'd thought the chalkboard was real too, so who knew?

But her teacher smiled. "Not terribly far," he answered. "Approximately eighty feet." A few of the other kids gulped, but Jules didn't have a problem with closed-in spaces or being underground. Heights were a totally different matter.

"Why're you wearing a tux?" Christopher asked

next. "This school doesn't have a dress code—I checked." Jules tried not to snicker at that. Given his clothes, she could see why he'd be worried!

"Hm? Oh, no," their teacher replied. "I've a state dinner to attend after, at the . . . well, I thought it'd just move things along quicker if I didn't have to head home and change."

A state dinner? Jules wondered about that. What would a science teacher be going to some fancy dinner somewhere? And why had he stopped himself from telling them where it was?

After a few more seconds the elevator slowed and then came to a stop so gently that it barely rocked everyone back on their feet. The doors slid open, and a small, hairy figure stood in front of them, gesturing wildly with long arms and gibbering like a crazy person.

Somebody screamed. Jules thought it was Ilyana. Or maybe Christopher. She kind of hoped it was Malik, though that was mean of her. She was a little startled herself and took a step back. Then she realized two things.

First, the creature standing there was just a chimpanzee. An older one, judging by all the white whiskers on his chin and around his eyes.

Second, he was wearing what looked like a blue flight suit. It had some kind of winged patch over its

27

left chest and a circle with the word "NASA" through it over the right, a U.S. flag on the left arm, and something she couldn't make out on the right arm.

NASA is the National Aeronautics and Space Administration. It is the United States government agency responsible for space travel as well as research about space and the Earth's upper atmosphere. NASA was created in 1958 as a nonmilitary agency looking into peaceful uses for space travel and space science.

Everything was making less sense by the second!

"Hello, Bud," Mr. Enright said to the chimp, sliding past the students and exiting the elevator first. "Sorry we're late. Pillai was being a pill, heh!" Sunita Pillai was the principal, Jules remembered. She was surprised to hear their teacher speak about her like that. Christopher, on the other hand, looked like he might be sick.

The chimp grunted and made more sounds in reply.

"I know, I know," Mr. Enright answered, almost as if he'd understood the small, blue-clothed primate. "It'll be fine, don't worry." Then he glanced back over his shoulder at the class. "So come along, let me show you the real classroom."

He took off down the hall, Bud loping along at his side, and Jules and the others hurried after them. The hall wasn't very long, and it ended at a wide door made from the same metal as the walls and the elevator. It slid open silently when the teacher approached, and he led them into something that looked more like what you'd see in the movies than in a school.

It had the same walls and floors as everything else behind that fake chalkboard so far. But there was a gleaming new whiteboard mounted on one wall and a row of large flat-screen monitors on another. Instead of desks, the room had tall, sort of oblong tables with wide, glossy tops and drawers along the sides and tall, padded black and chrome stools arranged around them. Each table had a sink to one side, a row of silvery nozzles on the opposite end, and a set of plugs grouped in the middle. Long counters that matched the tables covered the other two walls, with kitchen-style cupboards below and glass-fronted cabinets above. Instead of the subdued lighting in the hall, there were fluorescent lights hanging around the room and what Jules thought were strange spotlights over each table, though she didn't see any bulbs in them. Weird.

"Welcome to STEM class 1," Mr. Enright announced, spreading his arms wide to take in the room. "Very nifty, am I right?"

"Super nifty," Ilyana agreed, gazing around her with bright eyes. "It's like something out of a sci-fi movie!"

"Or a comic book," Malik muttered. He didn't sound quite as impressed—not completely unimpressed, maybe, but not totally dazzled, either. "So what's the deal with all this, anyhow? Why hide this super-cool space from everybody else? And what's with the really short security guard?" He gestured at Bud, who chittered back at him like he was angry about the crack. But he couldn't have understood it, could he?

"Do you all know what STEM is?" Mr. Enright asked, heading to the front of the class and perching on a stool there. Christopher's hand shot up.

"It stands for Science, Technology, Engineering, and Mathematics," he explained once the teacher had nodded toward him. "It's an educational program that shows how those subjects are all related. Math can be really boring in class, but it can be pretty cool when you use it with engineering or technology. Like designing a suspension bridge or whatever."

A **suspension bridge** is a kind of bridge in which the deck hangs from vertical cables that are attached to suspension cables, which are attached to towers rooted deep into the ground. The Brooklyn Bridge in New York City was the first steel-wire suspension bridge and was built in 1883.

"Very good, Christopher," their teacher agreed, which made the boy beam. "And this is a new experimental class where we'll focus on STEM." He leaned back, elbows going onto the counter on either side behind him, looking totally relaxed. "The five of you were selected because you each scored extremely well on those science evaluations you took yesterday. Yet, according to your teachers here and at your old schools, none of you are enthused about math and science." Mr. Enright looked at all of them. "We're going to change that."

None of the kids looked entirely thrilled with this idea. "And what about the monkey?" Malik asked. "Is he your teaching aide?" That earned him another rebuke from Bud, who chattered angrily, clacking his wide, square teeth together and making Malik shrink back a little. Jules tried hard not to giggle. Malik Jamar, intimidated by a chimp! Bet he wouldn't be tweeting about that!

"No, the teaching aide should be here tomorrow. Bud's more of a colleague," Mr. Enright answered easily. "He doesn't work here—that would be illegal and against all sorts of health codes, probably! But he'll be around a lot. And you should show him some respect, too. He used to work for NASA."

"Was he an astronaut?" Jules asked, eyeing the chimp's flight suit. It certainly looked real!

An **astronaut** is a person who has been trained to serve onboard a spacecraft. The term is sometimes used for anyone who has traveled into space, but more often it applies to those whose job is to go into space. In Russia, such a person is called a cosmonaut.

"He was," their teacher replied. "You'll find mentions of him online if you look him up. He got too old for the program—they're terribly strict about that because space travel does a real number on you physically—and he was going stir-crazy just sitting around all day, so now he'll be helping out around here from time to time. Don't worry, he—"

He stopped mid-sentence as an alarm sounded from the wall of monitors. Everyone started at the sudden sound, but Bud was the first to react. Racing past the students, the chimp rushed over to the monitors and began punching buttons on a console below them. Then he turned and hurried back, clambered up onto the counter next to Mr. Enright, grabbed the teacher's head with both hands, and pulled Mr. Enright in so he could whisper in his ear.

"What?" Mr. Enright asked. He listened a bit more. "Really? Yes, yes." Rising to his feet, the teacher gestured for the class to stand as well. "It appears we have a small situation in the boiler room," he explained, marching toward the door out into the hall. "Grab your bags and come on!"

"Boiler room?" Ilyana asked Jules as they all traipsed onto the elevator. "As in, the school basement?"

Jules shrugged. She had no more idea than the rest of them. Nor did she know why, if there was something going on in the school's boiler room, Mr. Enright thought he should take his class there.

And what had Bud been doing on that console, anyway? Apparently he really was smart!

Once they'd reached Room 103, Mr. Enright led them all down the hall and to a door off the central corridor. That proved to be a narrow flight of stairs going back down somewhere. Judging by how dark the stairway was, and how the stairs were nothing but plain gray metal, it didn't look like it was really intended for use by students.

"If the boiler room is downstairs, and we were

already underground, why didn't we go straight from our classroom to there?" Tracey asked as they all took the stairs, clutching the single metal handrail built into the wall for support and guidance. "Wouldn't that have been faster?"

"Possibly," Mr. Enright called back over his shoulder. He was in the lead, and Bud was bringing up the rear. "Unfortunately, we haven't had the time to connect the lab to the rest of the school—that would've required digging all the way under and then adding new reinforcements to the foundations to make up for the fact that we'd cleared out some of the rock and dirt everything was resting on. It was far quicker and easier to just attach it to the end of the furthest wing, which is why it's built below 103. Watch your step!"

The stairs ended at a solid metal fire door, which Mr. Enright ushered everyone through.

The first thing Jules noticed was that it was hot down here. Really hot. Like, almost scalding. That was presumably because of the boiler or furnace or whatever.

The second thing she noticed was that there wasn't a whole lot of light, just a handful of bare bulbs strung along the ceiling at intervals. Creepy.

The third thing was that she could hear water. Not the rainfall from outside, either. This sounded more like someone had twisted a faucet tap all the way to high, and water was spraying out of it into a sink or shower or tub.

"Hello?" Mr. Enright called. "Anyone here? Mr. Carruthers?"

"Who's that?" A figure emerged from the far end of the room. It was an older man, broad across the shoulders like a football player, with graying hair and beard. He was wearing a gray baseball cap and a grease-stained coverall that was soaked below the knees, at the wrists, and across the chest. "Who're you?"

"I'm Mr. Enright," their teacher introduced himself. "These are my students from STEM class 1. What seems to be the problem?" The contrast between their teacher, in his elegant tuxedo, and the janitor, in his stained coverall, was like night and day. Jules could only imagine how it looked to Mr. Carruthers, having such a fancily dressed man and a bunch of kids barge into his domain!

"The problem?" The janitor scowled at them. Jules saw that he was clenching a large wrench in one hand. "The problem is, the darn pipe just burst! Water's everywhere! And if it hits the furnace, we're gonna have a steam cloud big enough to swallow the school!"

"Hmmm." Mr. Enright turned to face the class.

"Very well, class," he said. "Here is your first real assignment. We've got a burst water pipe. What do we do?"

At first they all just gaped at him. What did they do? They were kids! How were they supposed to know? But Mr. Enright waited patiently, and finally Tracey offered, "Turn off the water?"

"Right, good first step," their teacher agreed. "Mr. Carruthers, I assume there's some reason you haven't done that yet?"

"Yeah, darn thing is rusted shut," the janitor answered with a grumble. He held up the wrench. "I've been trying, but it won't budge."

"Right. Clearly we have to get it unstuck," Mr. Enright clarified. "Anyone have any notions on how to do that?"

"We could apply more force," Jules suggested. "Like all of us pulling at once."

"We could spray it with some kind of oil," Malik said. "That might get it moving again."

Tracey had a different solution. "Bang on it," she stated. When the others turned to look at her, she shrugged. "Sometimes you gotta bang on it to shake it loose," she explained.

"Let's try all three," Mr. Enright told them. "We'll use oil to loosen it, and bang on it to shake things free a bit, then all try tugging together. Sound like a plan?"

Everyone agreed, and he rubbed his hands together. "Excellent! Mr. Carruthers, show us to the water cutoff, please."

The janitor muttered a bit but finally did as he was asked, guiding them to a thick pipe that rose from the ground before branching off into several smaller pipes. It was one of those smaller ones that was spraying water everywhere. "There y'are," he declared, gesturing toward the shorter pipe and indicating the valve visible on its side just above the floor. "Good luck." He set the wrench down and then stepped back, arms folded, to watch what happened next.

"Right!" Mr. Enright enthused. "Do we have any oil?" Mr. Carruthers stalked off and returned a minute or two later with a small spray can of machine oil. "Perfect!" Mr. Enright offered the container to Malik. "That one was your idea, Malik," the teacher pointed out, "so I'll let you do the honors." Jules wondered if that was also partially because Mr. Enright didn't want to risk getting oil all over his tuxedo, but their teacher didn't seem at all concerned about the rest of the dirt and grime down here, so maybe not.

Malik took the can carefully—he seemed a lot more worried about his clothes than Mr. Enright did about his—then approached the valve, trying to duck under the worst of the spray. He crouched down to get closer and angled the can before spraying the valve liberally. "That should help," he said, rising and moving clear again.

Next Mr. Enright handed the wrench to Tracey, who took it, closed in on the valve, and then whacked it hard with the wrench head. The pipe gave off a loud clang, and the whole area around the valve shook. A spray of red dust rose from it as well. "Rust," Tracey said with a nod. "That's a good sign that it's been knocked loose."

She passed the wrench to Jules, who placed it around the valve and then tightened the head until it had a firm grip. She grasped the wrench handle with both hands, and Tracey added hers as well. The others also latched on as best they could. "On the count of three!" Jules called out. "One! Two! Three!"

They all yanked together. At first nothing happened. Then, with a hideous screech that tore at their ears, the valve began to move. Slowly at first, then faster and more easily as it shifted out of its rusted position, it cycled to the side, and above it, the spray of water slowed to a trickle and then stopped completely.

"Huh," was all Mr. Carruthers said, pushing back his cap to scratch at his forehead, but Jules could tell he was impressed.

Mr. Enright was more effusive. "Brilliant job, class!" he enthused as he offered the janitor his wrench back. "That's what STEM is all about! You studied the problem, considered possible solutions, and decided on a course of action!" He led them back toward the stairs as he continued talking. "Now, you got lucky and your first solution worked. That's not always going to be the case—a lot of the time, you'll have to stop, reevaluate, figure out what went wrong with the first plan, and then modify it so you can try again. It helped that this time you had three separate solutions that could be combined into a single larger approach."

They returned to the main hall just as the last bell sounded. "For tomorrow," Mr. Enright told them, "think about what we did down there. What if that hadn't worked? What would you have tried next? How else could you have taken care of the problem?" He beamed at them. "Good work today! See you tomorrow!"

Jules couldn't help smiling as she headed to her locker. That had been kind of amazing! They'd fixed a leak in the school—and they'd done it themselves, just the five of them, with no real help from their teacher or the school janitor or anybody else! How sick was that?

It was true that she'd never cared much about science, but she was starting to think that maybe she just hadn't given it a proper chance.

CHAPTER 4

RECONSIDERING

That night, Malik sat in his room thinking about the homework Mr. Enright had assigned. How would he have fixed the problem of the boiler room leak if closing that valve hadn't worked? He had no idea.

It was still pouring out, which didn't exactly help his concentration. The sound of the rain pattering overhead was soothing, and now that he'd eaten and it was dark out, Malik just wanted to wash up, get into bed, and let the storm lull him to sleep. He couldn't do that, though, until he'd gotten all of his homework done for the night. And the one that was stumping him was the STEM assignment. He'd been staring at his computer screen for half an hour trying to come up with ideas, but he was drawing a blank. This was a whole heck of a lot harder than just reading some chapter!

A knock on the door made him look up. "Yeah?"

His dad stuck his head in. "Everything okay?"

"Sure." Malik sighed. "No. I'm trying to do my homework, but I'm stuck."

"What's the problem?" His father came all the way into the room and leaned against Malik's desk. One great thing about his dad was that, even though he was a lawyer and was always bringing work home himself, he still made time to talk to Malik and his younger sister, Nadira, to see how their days went and if they needed help with their work or anything.

"I need to figure out ways to take care of a leaky pipe," Malik explained. "Without turning off the valve."

His father frowned. "That's an odd homework assignment. What class is this for, again?"

"STEM class," Malik answered. "We're learning how to apply science, technology, engineering, and math to real-world problems."

"Oh. Well, that makes sense." His dad was a very practical guy. "Okay, so you've got a leaky pipe, and you can't shut the water off at the valve?" He scratched his chin. "Did your teacher give you any advice?"

Malik thought about that. "Not about this assignment," he answered finally, "but he did say that in general we should be considering the problem, looking at all our possible solutions, and then deciding on a course of action."

His dad nodded. "That sounds like a good approach. Go with that." He patted Malik on the shoulder. "Think about everything that's going on in the situation," he suggested. "Look at everything you have on hand to solve the problem and everything that could be affecting it. That should give you something to work with." That was something else about his father—he never gave them the answers to their homework, but he was happy to suggest things that could lead them to figuring out those answers for themselves. He said that, this way, they were actually learning rather than just copying down something he told them. Malik understood why, but it was still frustrating sometimes.

Right now, though, his dad's suggestion gave him the push he needed. Opening up a blank document on his computer, Malik started noting everything he remembered seeing in the boiler room and everything that was around the leak in particular. Then he went down the list and considered each element in turn. What was there that he could use? What might have some effect on the situation? There were lots of things that didn't factor in at all, like the furnace or the sink. It was mainly the pipe that had the actual leak, and the pipe that it sprang from above the valve, and then the boiler it led to. Malik couldn't go for the valve, and the boiler was past the problem area, so he'd have to focus on the pipe itself. But without turning the water off completely, what could he do?

He considered searching for answers online but decided that would be cheating. The goal here was to figure it out for himself. So what tools did he have on hand? Maybe that would help suggest a solution. There was the wrench, of course—could he use that somehow? But what good would a wrench do if you weren't trying to turn something that was stuck? He could clamp it over the spot that was leaking, but unless it was airtight, the water would still spray out all around the wrench, so that wasn't much help.

Now, if there was a way to shut off the water in the pipe without using the valve, that might work. Malik considered that. Like installing a new valve along the damaged pipe, in a way. You'd have to lock down on the pipe so tightly that the water couldn't force its way through to the break. The wrench couldn't do that—but a clamp could. Or a vise grip.

He wrote that down. Then he drew a diagram to show how it would fit. Would it work? He had no idea. But it sounded like a good option to try if the thing with the valve hadn't worked, so that was what he'd suggest tomorrow.

Relieved, Malik turned to the little bit of homework he had from his other classes. Then he set out clothes for the next day and went to bed. He was a little nervous about how his proposed solution would go over, but he was excited to talk about it too, and to see what his classmates had come up with.

"So, do you think we should just wait around here for Mr. Enright to show, or should we go ahead downstairs without him?" Christopher asked anxiously the next day. Malik had reached 103 to discover the other boy already pacing in front of the windows. Water slid down them from the rain outside, which had barely let up since the previous morning. Malik's father had said on the drive over that if this continued, there would probably be flooding, but he'd assured Malik that their house was on a hill so they would be fine. They'd had to detour around a few streets, however, that were already looking dangerous to cross.

"No idea," Malik answered now. He glanced up at the clock. Technically they were still within the five-minute grace period between classes. "Why don't we wait until the bell? He might show up, and so might the others."

Christopher nodded and sank into one of the desk chairs, but he immediately popped back to his feet. Malik studied the other boy as he resumed pacing. He noticed that Christopher was wearing a different band shirt today, and that he was tapping his fingers against his leg in a complicated rhythm. "So you're a musician, right?" Malik asked finally.

"Yeah," Christopher answered. He gave a little grin. "It's that obvious, huh?"

"Just a bit," Malik replied, smiling back. "I'm a little surprised, though. Yesterday you seemed a bit . . . focused on the whole grades thing."

His classmate shrugged, looking a little embarrassed. "That's the deal," he admitted after a minute. "With my parents. I've got to get straight As or I'm out of my band."

"Ouch." Now Malik could see why he'd be so worried about a class that didn't seem to have a grading structure. "Sorry, dude."

"Yo," Tracey called as she entered the room. "Where's the chimp?"

Jules was right behind her. "Probably planning his next attack on Malik," she said, chuckling. "You'd better watch out, Malik—Bud's got your number."

"Not to worry," Malik replied, trying not to show how annoyed he was by her crack—or how nervous. "I've got it covered." The others studied him curiously, but he just smirked and refused to say any more. They'd see.

"Sorry I'm late," Ilyana said as she rushed in. "I was trying to finish reading this." She held up a comic book. Malik couldn't make out the title, but it had a picture of men in space suits on the cover. It seemed like Ilyana spent all of her time reading.

"So," she continued, flicking back her long hair, "Does anybody else think yesterday was epic?"

Tracey beamed. "Totally!"

"Yeah, but what's up with this class?" Malik asked them. "I mean, there's only five of us. What kind of a class is that?"

"He did say it was an experiment," Christopher said. "We're like, test subjects or something."

"Oh, that's comforting!" Tracey replied. "So what, we're lab rats now?"

"I didn't even tell my parents what went on yesterday," Malik admitted to his classmates. "I figured they'd never believe me!" Who would, really? A secret lab, a teacher who wore a tux, a chimp, and a trip to the boiler room? It was like some bad movie or something. Only, this was his life!

"No sign of the teacher," Christopher announced, studying his watch. "And it's time for class to start. Should we wait here or head down?"

"Why wait?" Jules asked. She stalked down the row, loping as she did on the basketball court, and passed through the fake blackboard without even a pause. The others shrugged and followed.

She must have already pushed the elevator button, because the doors were open when everyone joined her. They filed in, and Ilyana, who had been last, pushed "C."

"What does that stand for, do you think?" she asked as the doors slid shut and the car began its descent. "Class?"

"Makes sense," Tracey agreed. "But what's the "S" for, then?"

It was Christopher who answered. "Surface," he suggested, and everyone agreed.

The elevator stopped with a faint shudder, and the doors opened. Bud was standing there waiting for them.

"Hi, Bud!" Jules called out. She held out a hand, palm up, and the chimp grinned and slapped it as she passed him. The others all waved and said hello as well.

Malik was the last one out. "I'm really sorry about yesterday," he told Bud. Then he held out the banana he'd retrieved from his backpack. "I hope this makes up for it."

Bud stared at him for a second. Then the chimp nodded and grabbed the banana. But then he reached out and wrapped one long arm around Malik's shoulders and tugged him down into a tight hug!

"Okay, okay," Malik said. He couldn't help laughing. "I'm glad we're friends."

The chimp smiled, showing all his teeth, and then

released Malik, took him by the hand, and led him down the hall to the classroom. Well, Malik thought as he let Bud drag him along, chattering the whole way, at least it's better than having him hate me!

"Hello, Malik," Mr. Enright said as they entered. "Glad you and Bud have made up." The teacher wasn't wearing a tux today, but rather a button-down shirt and jeans. A sport coat hung from a hook on the wall.

"Yessir," Malik agreed, taking a seat at one of the tables next to Ilyana. Tracey and Jules were at another, and Christopher was by himself at the table in front.

"Right, attendance." Their teacher turned to his clipboard and ran his finger down it, calling off each name in turn. "Ilyana Desoff, Tracey DeGuerra, Malik Jamar, Julie Robbins, Christopher Wong—excellent!" Then he set the clipboard aside and settled onto the same stool he'd claimed yesterday, facing the rest of them.

"Now, let's talk about your homework."

CHAPTER 5

FRESH EYES

"Right," Mr. Enright said. "What'd you all come up with?"

The rest of the day had gone fine, even if the constant rain and continual gray skies had cast a pall over everything and everyone. But Jules had been excited to see what everyone had come up with for the homework. She herself had hit on what she had hoped was both a clever way to deal with the problem and something no one else had thought of, and so she raised her hand, eager to present it before anyone else said the same thing.

"Yes, Jules?" Mr. Enright said, calling on her. "How would you have fixed the pipe if that valve hadn't worked?"

"Liquid nitrogen," she answered at once, bouncing up onto her feet. "I'd have frozen the pipe, and the water coming out of it. That'd work like a plug and seal the leak until I could have the valve fixed and the damaged section properly replaced."

Nitrogen is a natural element. At room temperature, it is a clear, odorless gas. Nitrogen can be cooled, however, and turned into a liquid. **Liquid nitrogen** has an extremely low temperature (between $-346°F$ and $-320°F$) and will freeze almost anything it touches upon contact. Liquid nitrogen is the preferred way to transport nitrogen because it does not require pressurization.

Their teacher considered that. "Interesting suggestion," he replied after some thought. "There's a risk, of course—you've got to be really careful with liquid nitrogen because you could destroy the entire pipe. Then again, it already has to be replaced, so that's not as much of a problem. The real question is whether the frozen area would be able to withstand the pressure from the water behind it. It's a clever idea, though, and at the very least it might keep things from getting worse while you figured something else out. Good work."

Jules sank back onto her stool, pleased. It might not be a perfect solution, but he'd still praised her quick thinking, and he was right—even if it only stopped the leak for a little while, that was something.

"What about the rest of you?" Mr. Enright asked the other students.

Malik had his answer ready. "I'd use a clamp to block the water from coming all the way down the pipe to the broken spot," he explained. "It'd be like adding a new valve, but farther up on the damaged section."

"Good," Mr. Enright agreed. "That could work. Again, you'd have to be careful if you were trying to avoid damaging the pipe any more, and the clamp would have to be able to tighten so thoroughly that no water could get past, but if you could do that you're right—you'd effectively block it from getting to that spot. Next?"

Tracey's solution was more direct, which didn't surprise Jules at all. She was already learning that her classmate and new friend took the direct approach, just like she did. Tracey was also mechanically minded, so she tended to think in terms of cars and machines and tools. Like now, when she suggested that they simply weld the damaged portion. "That way you'd actually fix the break or crack or whatever it was, so you wouldn't have to worry about water getting through again." She frowned. "You couldn't do that with the water still coming out, though, so you'd need something like Malik's solution or Jules's first, in order to dry out the damaged pipe before you tried welding it."

Their teacher nodded. "Very true. And, just like yesterday, you are seeing how sometimes your solution is only part of the whole answer, and by working together you can really fix the problem quickly and completely."

Just then the door opened, and in marched a man. That was Jules's first thought, at least.

As he approached, however, she realized that he wasn't a man. Not really. He was a boy, maybe a few years older than them, about her height. He was in good shape, though, which was clearly evident through the tight black T-shirt he was wearing. He also had on a black cap and black pants with black combat boots, but unlike Christopher's boots, this guy's practically shone in the lab's light.

"Sir!" the new boy announced, coming to a sharp stop right in front of Mr. Enright—had he just clicked his heels together?—and saluting. Saluting? Really? "Warner, Randall, reporting for duty, sir!"

"Ah, yes," Mr. Enright replied, studying the newcomer. "You're the teacher's aide. Good to meet you, lad." He gave what might have been a wave but could have been a very lazy return salute as well. Whatever it was, it seemed to satisfy Randall. "At ease, son," the teacher added, and their new teacher's aide relaxed his rigid stance slightly, his feet moving apart a little and hands going behind his back.

"Sorry I'm late, sir," Randall barked out, staring straight ahead. "Had to report to the principal first— commanding officer and all that."

"Yes, yes, that's fine," Mr. Enright assured him. "Meet the class: Ilyana, Tracey, Malik, Jules, and Christopher." He gestured at each of them as he said their names. "Class, this is Randall, our teacher's aide. He'll be assisting me."

"It's an honor, sir," Randall declared, still staring at the far wall. He hadn't moved since he'd settled into his current pose.

"Are you in the military?" Ilyana blurted out. "You look like you're in the military."

Randall's chest puffed out a bit. "ROTC, junior year," he replied with obvious pride. "Navy. Gonna be a SEAL—if I make the grade." Now that he'd said that, Jules realized that his belt was a military-style canvas clasp and had what she thought might be the U.S. Navy symbol on its buckle.

"Are you a science major?" she asked. She was trying to figure out Randall, who was so obviously a career military guy, would be doing here.

"No, ma'am," he answered, still not looking at her or any of them. "Chemical engineering." A small smirk cracked his lips. "Demolitions."

A **demolition** is the practice of tearing down buildings and other structures, typically with the use of explosives. The goal in demolition is to destroy the target as quickly, cleanly, and thoroughly as possible.

"Oh." Well, that made some sense, then. Still, his presence just added to the oddity that was this class.

For a moment after that, nobody spoke. Mr. Enright was just leaning back, evidently totally at ease, surveying them, while Randall still did his best impression of a statue—or at least an action figure—and Jules and her new classmates sat there, trying to figure out what was going to happen next.

"Excuse me, sir?" Christopher asked finally, raising his hand.

Mr. Enright laughed lightly. "No need to raise your hand, Christopher," he replied, leaning back. "We're not all that formal around here. What is it?"

"Can you tell us what this class is going to entail?" Christopher continued. Jules noticed that the other boy had a notebook out and open, and a pen poised over the page. "Will there be a syllabus? A textbook? Are there going to be quizzes? Tests? Reports? How will we be graded?" Each question had come out with more urgency, and the last one burst from him with the force of a cannon. Jules shook her head. He was really fixated on the whole grades thing!

But their teacher didn't seem to mind. He only chuckled again. "I'll let you know as soon as I figure it out," he promised. Christopher looked like someone had just told him there wasn't a Santa Claus. "As I said yesterday, this is an experimental class," Mr.

Enright explained, leaning forward. "I'm still working out some of the details. For now, let's start by talking about science in general, okay?"

He hopped up off his stool and began walking around the room, making the kids twist in their own seats to follow his motion. "What is science, exactly?" Mr. Enright asked. Christopher's hand shot up at once. "Yes?" their teacher acknowledged him.

Christopher sat straight as a ruler. "Science is the study of something in an organized and logical fashion," he recited, "relying upon experiments and tests for verification." It was obvious he'd read that somewhere and memorized it, probably last night. Jules had spent last night doing some basketball drills in the driveway, listening to a new song by an artist she liked, and texting a friend who had gone to a different high school to compare first week stories.

"Yes, very good," their teacher said. "If you're a textbook." That got laughs from the others, but Christopher turned a bit red, even though Mr. Enright's tone was playful rather than scolding. "But you're correct, science is a way of studying something. You can study the world around us, which includes the natural sciences like biology and chemistry. You can study people, which are the social sciences like anthropology and archaeology. Or you can study abstract things, which are the formal sciences like mathematics and statistics." He paused and looked around the room, then smiled. "And I'm guessing, from most of your faces, that the idea of science doesn't exactly thrill you."

Biology is the basic study of life and all living organisms.
Chemistry is the study of chemicals (such as elements like oxygen and nitrogen), their qualities and uses, and the changes they undergo—such as how to combine them.
Anthropology is the study of man, mainly by examining human society, both past and present.
Archaeology is the study of humanity's past, specifically by examining ruins, artifacts, and other remnants of previous times in history.
Statistics is the study of data and how to organize and interpret it. Statistics can be used to predict the likelihood of any particular event.

CHAPTER 6

WHAT IT ALL MEANS

Nobody answered at first. But finally Tracey muttered, "What's the point?"

Mr. Enright turned toward her. "That's a fair question," he replied, not sounding offended at all. Malik thought that the new guy, Randall, looked ready to read her the riot act, though. Was that because he loved science so much, Malik wondered, or because Tracey had mouthed off—sort of—to their teacher? "Let's explore that. What is the point? Why do we study science?"

Again, Christopher raised his hand. Then he seemed to remember what Mr. Enright had said about not being that formal. "So that we can learn more about the world around us?" he offered after a second.

"Certainly," their teacher agreed. "But how often do you really use science? That's what you meant, right?" he asked Tracey, who nodded. "After all, how often do you need biology? Or chemistry? Or physics? Or geology?" Mr. Enright had begun walking again as he talked, and now he was back in the front of the room. Oddly, Randall had broken from his pose to shadow the teacher, marching along a few paces behind him. "Well, let's answer that," their teacher suggested, perching on his stool again. Randall once again took up his previous stance, in exactly the same spot as before, as far as Malik could tell. "Why would you use, let's say, chemistry?"

"If you were mixing an antidote for some poison?" Ilyana offered.

An **antidote** is a substance designed to counter a poison or some other harmful substance, particularly one that has been swallowed, injected, or inhaled.

Mr. Enright laughed. "Sure, though let's hope you don't have to do that too often, right? I mean, the school lunches aren't that bad, are they?" The kids all laughed along with him, including Ilyana. At least she didn't have a problem poking fun at herself, Malik thought. "What else? When would you use chemistry?"

"If you were trying to mix cleaning solution?" Tracey asked.

"Absolutely," their teacher agreed. "But let's go for something a little more basic and a lot more common. Do any of you ever get sick? Cold, flu, things like that?"

They all acknowledged that they had. It was almost impossible not to get something from time to time, especially in school. Malik washed his hands before and after every meal and carried a small container of hand sanitizer as well, but even so, you were bound to touch something at some point, and all it took was one contagious kid to spread that around the whole school.

"So when you're sick, your parents give you medicine, yes?" Mr. Enright continued. "Well, that's chemistry—those medicines are either natural substances like aspirin or elderberry, or they're manmade, like acetaminophen or diphenhydramine."

Aspirin, or acetylsalicylic acid, is a medicine used for dealing with pain (particularly headaches and joint pain), fever, and inflammation. It can also help reduce the effects of a heart attack and lower the risk of blood clots. It was first discovered in willow tree bark.
Acetaminophen is an analgesic, meaning it is a medicine primarily used for pain relief. It is most commonly taken to deal with headaches and minor aches and pains. It is also often found in cold and flu medicine.
Diphenhydramine is a medicine most often taken for allergies. It is an antihistamine, meaning that it suppresses swelling and dilation in the nose and lungs, making it easier to breathe.

Jules surprised Malik by speaking up. "But that's not really us using chemistry, is it?" she asked. "I mean, those are chemicals, sure, but somebody already made them or combined them or whatever. We're just taking them."

"Fair enough, but what if you take more than one?" their teacher replied. "Let's say you've got a cold, you're stuffed up, your throat is sore, and you've got a headache. Your parents aren't home yet, and so you go into the medicine cabinet yourself. There's Benadryl there, that's diphenhydramine. There's Tylenol, that's acetaminophen. There's Advil, that's ibuprofen. And there's Sudafed, that's pseudoephedrine. So which one do you take?"

Ibuprofen is an anti-inflammatory drug, meaning that it reduces swelling. It is used to relieve pain and lower fevers.
Pseudoephedrine is a drug that functions as a decongestant (meaning it clears stuffiness and congestion from the nose, throat, and lungs). It is also a stimulant (meaning it increases alertness and wakefulness) and is carefully regulated by the FDA.

"All of them?" Ilyana suggested, but Malik was already shaking his head.

"You can't take them all together," he corrected her. "Tylenol and Advil do the same stuff, but they're not the same so you alternate them—you can only take each of them every four to six hours, but you can swap them out so you take one and then a few hours later take the other. Sudafed's for your nose. Benadryl's for your throat, but it's really for allergies, not colds—it probably won't help much if you've got a cold. So you start with Sudafed and either Tylenol or Advil—that'll cover your headache and your stuffiness, and between the two of them they'll probably make your throat feel better." His little sister, Nadira, had had a nasty cold over the summer, and at one point Malik's mom had been called away to the pharmacy where she worked, so she'd gone over everything with Malik before she left him in charge of caring for his sister. He was a little surprised he remembered so much of it.

He was also a little flustered, though pleased, when Mr. Enright clapped for him. "Excellent!" the teacher stated. "Very well done, Malik! You see, you're practically a chemist already!" Everyone laughed, though not meanly, as their teacher continued. "But seriously, that is using chemistry—and very well, too. You know which chemicals affect you in what ways, which ones do the same things, and which can be used together. That's really important. So even though you didn't make the medicines yourself, you still have to understand them in order to use them properly."

This time it was Christopher who spoke. "Okay, so that's the science portion of the class," he said slowly, "but what about the technology, engineering, and mathematics parts? Will we be doing them as sections and spend a few weeks on each one? With a quiz or a paper at the end of each and then a midterm and a final?" It was clear he was still desperate to give the class a familiar structure so he could start studying for something!

"Those four aren't as separate as all that," Mr. Enright answered, "so I suspect we'll be dealing with more than one of them at a time rather than taking them in turn. But we'll see. I'm a lot less concerned about tests and papers than I am about you learning to really appreciate what you can do with them, to be honest." Again, Christopher's face fell, and Mr. Enright laughed. "But I can assign you some reports and papers and things if it'll make you happy," he offered. Everyone else grumbled, but Christopher cheered up at once at the thought.

"I think that's enough for today," Mr. Enright said, glancing at the clock on the far wall. Malik twisted to look at it and was surprised to see that class was almost over. How had that happened? It felt like they'd just gotten down here! "Tell you what, I'll even give you a little homework," their teacher added. "But don't worry, it's not too strenuous. I just want you to go around your house tonight and think about all the ways you use science, technology, engineering, and math every day. Sound good? Oh, yes, and there are permission forms. Bud, would you pass those out, please?"

Suddenly Bud was there—had he been there all along? Malik hadn't noticed after they'd all sat down. The chimp grabbed a pile of papers from the counter. Then he leaped up onto the table the kids had

clustered around and started handing each of them a
form. When he got to Malik, though, Bud pulled the
papers away and puckered up his lips instead, leaning
forward.

"Ew, no, I am not giving you a kiss!" Malik
declared, putting up his hands to keep the chimp's face
from his own. "Stop that! Just give me a form!"

Everyone laughed, and Bud relented, handing him
one—but not before making a loud raspberry at him
first.

"I'm sorry," Malik told him. "I didn't mean to
hurt your feelings. But you're really not my type."

Bud grunted and slapped Malik on the back, so
hopefully that meant he was forgiven.

"Please have your parents sign those forms
tonight," Mr. Enright told them once Malik had his
safely in hand. "Then we can get started in earnest
tomorrow. Right? See you then!" Their teacher didn't
move, and neither did Randall—and why hadn't Mr.
Enright asked Randall to hand out the forms, Malik
wondered, since he was supposedly the teaching aide—
but Bud hopped down to the floor and led the way
back out into the hall, reaching up with his long arms
to push the elevator button. It opened at once, and
he gestured them in, reached around to push the "S"
button, and waved good-bye.

"That was the weirdest thing ever," Malik muttered once the elevator had closed and started up.

"Weird but cool!" Ilyana said. "I love it!"

"I'd still prefer more details on how the class will be structured," Christopher complained, frowning as he carefully folded the form and placed it in his backpack. "And how we'll be graded." He shrugged. "Still, it was interesting."

"Beats regular science class," Tracey agreed.

Oh, it's definitely interesting, Malik thought, listening to his new classmates talk. Things definitely weren't going to be dull down there in their secret lab, with tux-wearing Mr. Enright and soldier-boy Randall and former astronaut-chimp Bud. Maybe even a little too interesting.

But then again, was it really possible to be *too* interesting?

CHAPTER 7

EVERYDAY USE

"Are you okay, sweetie?" Jules's mom asked her at dinner that night. Jules had been staring at her food for a good minute or so.

"Hm? Oh, fine, Mom. Sorry," Jules answered absently. "Just thinking." She glanced down at the notebook she had open on the table beside her plate. They were having spaghetti and meatballs with garlic bread tonight. Did any of that count as science? There was sauce—was that a form of chemistry, figuring out which ingredients to mix together? The garlic bread had been toasted in the oven, the spaghetti had been boiled in a pot, the meatballs had been baked—cooking was a science, wasn't it? Heat and boiling points and things like that? She was so confused! But she wrote it all down anyway, just in case.

"They give you so much work you've got to do it during dinner?" her brother Trey teased. He was a senior in high school and thought he knew it all. Their older brother, Sly, was in college on a football scholarship, though he was technically working on a business degree.

Jules explained the homework assignment. "I'm not sure what counts and what doesn't, so I'm writing down anything that might apply," she finished. She'd already scribbled a whole bunch of things since she'd gotten home.

"That's a pretty cool assignment," her dad commented from the head of the table. "So this is some kind of special class? It's not going to weigh you down, is it?"

"No, it's fine," Jules answered quickly. Her dad was really big on sports—he'd played football and baseball in high school and college—and worried about anything that would distract her or her brothers from their games. But even though it was only the second day, she was really enjoying STEM class.

Admittedly, she was used to having a lot more structure. That's how sports worked, after all—there were rules and guidelines for everything. Still, it was kind of awesome how Mr. Enright seemed less worried about rules than about actually teaching them something. And the conversation today had been eye-opening too. Jules hadn't realized just how much science affected everything.

She also had to admit that she'd been really impressed with Malik. How had he known all that about different types of medicine? He'd always seemed like the kid who just breezed through on charm, but maybe that wasn't really fair to judge him.

Still thinking about class that day, Jules speared a meatball on her fork. Then she hefted her knife and sliced it in half. Hey, she thought. That's geometry, which is math!

Shoving the still-impaled half of meatball in her mouth, she wrote that down. Who knew dinner could be so mathematical—or that math could be so much fun and delicious?

Geometry is the study of shapes, particularly their properties and position and relation to one another.

The next day, Jules was eager to share her list with the class. The list kept growing, too. Like when she glanced outside, studying the rain clouds that were still looming overhead, even though the rain had stopped for the moment. Would it start raining again? she wondered. Probably—she'd better wear her poncho and rain boots, just in case. Then she giggled. That was meteorology! It went on the list!

The rain did start up again, even before Jules got to school. And it continued throughout the day, making the whole world dim and gray and filling the air with the steady beat of the rain drumming down on the school's roof. When she and the others gathered in

103 and then headed down to the lab, it was almost eerie how silent the underground space was by comparison.

Their teacher was already down there when they arrived. So was Randall, who immediately snapped, "Students, in your seats!" once they'd walked in. Startled by the sudden command, Jules glanced over at Mr. Enright, who just nodded. So she sat, as did the others. It wasn't like she hadn't been planning to sit down anyway, but did the new aide really need to shout at them?

Then Randall produced the class roster and proceeded to take roll, barking out their names like this was boot camp and he was the drill sergeant. It was a little annoying, but also kind of funny, so Jules decided to roll with it as best she could. She did roll her eyes, though. Tracey, who was sitting next to her, noticed and laughed.

"How did everyone do with the homework?" Mr. Enright asked after Randall had finished and handed him the roster. "Come up with any good lists? Anything that surprised you?"

Ilyana held up her hand. "I wear contacts," she stated, which didn't seem to connect to the question until she added, "I have to wash them out with saline every night. That's chemistry!"

"Absolutely," their teacher agreed. "Good job! Anybody else?"

Jules hesitated before speaking up. "We had spaghetti and meatballs last night," she started. "And I cut my meatballs in half so they'd be easier to chew. That's geometry, changing the shape of them."

"Good catch!" Mr. Enright said approvingly. "And what about the act of cutting them? What do you use for that?"

"Physics!" Christopher burst out, tapping his fingers on the table. "That's all about force and pressure and resistance! Any time we move anything, we're using physics!"

Their teacher laughed, clearly pleased with Christopher's enthusiasm. "It certainly is," he said. "Any time you mix two liquids together it's chemistry, any time you move something it's physics, and any time you calculate angles or shapes it's geometry. What else?" He glanced over at Tracey, who hadn't said anything. "Tracey? Anything to add? Any sciences we haven't touched on yet?"

"Um," she started. "Well, my mom had a headache last night, so I made her some tea. It's herbal mint and makes her feel better. That's botany, right?"

"Botany!" Mr. Enright almost shouted, as if it was the greatest thing ever. Everybody laughed. Now who was being enthusiastic? "Yes! Very good! Malik?"

Malik thought about it for a moment. Then he perked up. "I recycled my trash after lunch," he said. "That's ecology. And last night I tried to figure out how to get my parents to let me stay up later than usual so I could watch a show I wanted to see. That's logic."

Physics is the study of energy and matter and how the two, in their various forms and states, interact and intersect. The study of motion is also part of physics.

Botany is the branch of biology that deals entirely with plants.

Ecology is a branch of biology dealing with the relationship between organisms and their environment. Most often, ecology focuses on humanity and how people interact with the world around them, as well as ways to improve that interaction.

Logic is the study of reasoning, its principles, and the methods of applying those principles in order to think in a rational and orderly fashion.

"Which is a formal science like math because it deals in the abstract," Mr. Enright confirmed. "Very good! And ecology is connected to both biology and chemistry."

He leaned back against the counter behind him and beamed. "This is exactly what I was talking about yesterday," he told them. "We use STEM all the time, every day. We just don't always realize it. But once you stop and think, you start seeing it everywhere—in everything we do. That's why it's so important."

"So this class is about learning to recognize where STEM shows up in our lives?" Christopher asked.

"Not exactly," Mr. Enright responded. "That's part of it, sure, but we're going to do a lot more than that. STEM class is really about hands-on experience. That's how you accept things as real and how you make them part of your own knowledge base—by actually getting out there and getting your hands dirty." He gestured around the room. "The reason we have this lab is because we're going to do a lot of class activities, experiments, and the like. We'll learn proper lab procedures—so yes, Christopher, there will be rules for that, and you can study them to your heart's content. We're going to do some engineering too, and that's a different skill set, though the two are connected. We're going to learn about science and the rest, but then we're going to apply what we've learned to real situations and develop real solutions. Just as we did the other day in the boiler room, helping poor Mr. Carruthers. We—"

Just then, Bud burst into the room. Randall immediately dropped into a crouch, facing the chimp, hands spread wide, as if he were going to attack. But Bud ignored both Randall and the kids as he ran over to Mr. Enright and climbed up onto the counter to whisper something in the teacher's ear.

"Really? Very well, let's see," Mr. Enright replied.

Pulling a small, sleek remote from a nearby drawer, the teacher aimed the device at the wall of monitors. They switched to life, a single picture blurring into focus on every screen simultaneously, and everyone stared, transfixed, at the man now facing them in every frame. He was wearing a suit and was seated at a desk, shuffling some papers in front of him as he spoke, and his words were quick and hurried. Behind his right shoulder was the logo for a local news station. Also behind him was an inset image showing a house with water lapping up as high as the bottom edge of its front windows.

"—flooding the San Remas valley," the man was saying as the sound kicked in, echoing slightly as it projected from each monitor at once. "Evacuation has been successful, and officials are already setting up roadblocks to keep anyone else from wandering into the dangerous area, even as they search for ways to block the water and prevent even more damage to the residential neighborhood. With current weather reports calling for continued rain through tomorrow at the earliest, however, the area's fate looks grim. Some people are calling for—"

"Right," Mr. Enright announced, clicking off the monitors. He tossed the remote onto the counter behind him as he hopped up from his stool. "Let's go."

Randall immediately straightened and saluted. "Sir,

yes sir," he shouted. "Class, on your feet, double-time!" This guy was too much!

"Go?" Tracey asked, even as she and the others also stood, gathered their bags, and turned to follow as their teacher and the teacher's aide led them out of the room. "Go where?"

Mr. Enright just beamed at them. "Field trip time!" he declared, heading for the elevator.

They all crowded in together, but the students stared at each other, and Jules was sure they all were thinking the same thing: A field trip? In the middle of the worst storm in recent history? Where exactly were they going? And what would it have to do with STEM class?

She was beginning to wish that her parents hadn't been so willing to sign that consent form!

CHAPTER 8

STEPPING OUTSIDE

"Where are we going, exactly?" Malik asked as Mr. Enright guided them all back into the elevator and upstairs.

"Like I said, it's a field trip," their teacher explained. Bud, who had tailed along after them, chattered and bobbed his head in agreement. The chimp took Malik's hand as if to reassure him, which Malik found both amusing and a little irritating. Did the chimp think he was worried? Or scared? He wasn't! He just didn't like not knowing what was going on.

They emerged from the elevator and Mr. Enright led them out of the classroom, but rather than turning left and heading back down the corridor toward the main hall, he turned right, heading toward the emergency exit. "Just like that time in Heathrow," the tall man muttered as he did something to the door and then pushed it open. Malik tensed, as did his classmates, anticipating the shrill alarm, but the door opened with barely more than a creak. Bud immediately pulled free from Malik and dashed out into the rain.

"What'd you do?" Tracey demanded, pushing forward to study both their teacher and the door he was now holding open just enough for them to feel droplets of rain lashing in through the narrow gap. "How'd you disable the alarm?"

"Oh, a simple enough trick," Mr. Enright answered absently. "The door relies on a sensor to indicate when it's open or closed. It's a basic closed circuit, and if you break the circuit, it reacts—in this case, by sounding the alarm." He shrugged. "I simply rerouted the circuit." He shifted to the side so they could see the door more clearly—along the frame he'd attached a small box, which had a tiny blinking light on it. "This way the door thinks it's still closed, even though it's not."

A **circuit** is a closed path, or loop, that starts and ends at the same place without any gap. In electronics, a circuit is a closed path that electricity travels through, and completing or breaking that path—finishing or interrupting the circuit—is what triggers a change, like turning a light on or off.

Randall, Malik noticed, had whipped out a small notepad and was jotting something down. Was the teacher's aide taking notes? Or collecting evidence? He was an odd one; that was for sure!

Tracey considered that for a second. "Cool," she decided finally.

Their teacher nodded his head slightly to acknowledge the compliment and then glanced out the door. "Should be pulling up any moment," he said softly. "Just as long as—"

"Mr. Enright!" The call echoed down the hall, causing him to freeze like a dog caught trying to steal food off the table. All of them turned to see a short, sturdy woman in a business suit striding quickly toward them. She looked familiar, and as she drew closer Malik recognized her. It was Doctor Pillai, their principal.

"Where exactly do you think you're going during school hours?" Doctor Pillai demanded as she reached them. Her gaze swept across Malik and his classmates. "You and your students," she amended. Randall was standing at attention and saluted her, but she ignored him.

"Oh, just out on a little field trip," Mr. Enright answered easily, but Malik thought their teacher suddenly looked tense. "All part of the syllabus, you remember. 'Unscheduled field trips as circumstances allow.'" He looked confident. "Their parents all signed the consent forms."

"Be that as it may," the principal countered, "do you really think that this is the kind of weather that invites a trip off school property with a group of minors, no matter how their parents have granted permission?"

"It's *exactly* the weather to invite such a thing," their teacher replied. "If not for the weather, there wouldn't be much point in the field trip." He stepped toward Doctor Pillai and leaned down so that he could speak to her more privately. Malik watched, frowning. Something about this was very familiar. But what?

"That's ridiculous!" The principal declared in response to whatever Mr. Enright had just told her. "And it can't possibly be safe!"

"Of course it is," their teacher insisted, and Malik jumped. That was it! It was their voices! He'd already realized that Mr. Enright had been the man Malik had overheard at lunch the first day, but Dr. Pillai had been the woman he'd been talking to! She'd been worried that it wasn't safe, and he'd claimed it was! And Mr. Enright had said something about STEM, so it must have been their class that he'd meant.

And what about it wasn't safe? It was just a little rain, wasn't it?

"I assure you, I will take every possible precaution," Mr. Enright declared, straightening and stepping back away from the woman. "Now if you'll excuse me, the bus is waiting for us." He reached for the emergency exit again, which had slid shut when he'd released it, and swung it wide. "Class, follow me!" he called out, and strode outside without another glance.

Malik looked at Jules and the others. They all glanced at each other, all clearly thinking the same thing. Should they follow him? Or should they stay here? Malik suspected if they chose to stay inside, where it was warm and dry and safe, Dr. Pillai wouldn't punish them for it. In fact, she would probably applaud them for it!

But if they didn't go now, they might never find out what Mr. Enright's field trip entailed.

And while it might not be entirely safe, Malik suspected it would, at the very least, be interesting.

Making the decision, he took a deep breath and then plunged out into the rain. Jules beat him to the door by half a step, and the others were right behind them.

The bus had indeed pulled up right by the exit door, so it was a matter of a few feet from the door to the bus's waiting entrance.

Malik was half-soaked by the time he swung up into the bus. Wow, it was really coming down!

"Glad you decided to join me," Mr. Enright said to Jules as she clambered aboard, turning around to extend that to all of them. Malik had the feeling their teacher knew exactly how close he'd come to losing his entire class. He didn't look at all concerned, though. Just pleased.

"Let's go, Bud," Mr. Enright said once Randall had clambered onboard, and for the first time, Malik realized that the chimp was sitting in the driver's seat. But the chimp was so short that his legs just dangled; they were nowhere near the pedals!

"Wait, Bud's driving?" Tracey asked. Bud smiled in response, clacking his teeth, and yanked on the door level, slamming the bus door shut. Then he pushed a button on the dash and the bus lurched into motion, throwing everyone else around as they all scrambled for seats.

"Certainly he's driving," Mr. Enright answered from the front seat, which he'd slid into without pause. "He's rated to handle Rovers on Mars and the moon; I think he can manage a school bus in Southern California."

Everyone stared at him for a minute until he laughed. "No, no, I'm only joking," he assured them. "Of course Bud isn't driving—he's a chimpanzee, for heaven's sake! Who would've given him a license?"

"But—" Ilyana started, then stopped. "If he's not driving," she tried again, "who is?"

"Oh, the bus is driving itself," Mr. Enright told her cheerfully. "It's the latest thing in automation, don't you know. Automotive automation, one could even say. Heh heh." He leaned back in his seat. "Bud's merely handling the controls, pushing the buttons, and whatnot." He shrugged. "He seems to enjoy it."

Malik sank back against his seat, shaking his head. They were going on a field trip. In a rainstorm. In a school bus driven by a chimpanzee—only it wasn't really, because the bus was actually driving itself.

Well, he'd been right—it was already pretty interesting!

Automation is using machinery to operate something or control something that would normally require human involvement, like a lawn mower that does not need anyone to steer it.

CHAPTER 9

DRIVING THE BUS

"Everyone buckle up!" Mr. Enright called over his shoulder as the school bus rumbled its way out of the school parking lot and onto the road beyond. "This could get a little bumpy!" Randall, of course, echoed the order and then began stomping up and down the short aisle, clearly intending to loom over each student until they complied.

Jules didn't wait for Randall to get to her. At the teacher's suggestion she'd reached up automatically, grasping the seat belt and pulling it across her, then buckling it in place. Normally, bus drivers didn't bother to tell kids to use their seat belts, but given the weather—and the fact that nobody was driving!—she thought it probably wasn't such a bad idea.

She'd just succeeded in clicking the lock into place when the school bus went rattling around a corner onto an intersecting street. There was a screech as the tires scraped against the asphalt, audible even over the storm, and a lurch as the two inner wheels left the ground for a second before thumping back down. Randall had to grab hold of two seats to keep from tumbling off his feet. The bus didn't even bother to slow down.

"Good job on the turn, bus!" Mr. Enright called out as if the bus could hear him. Bud seemed to think the compliment had been meant for him, because he grunted and grinned and gripped the steering wheel. At least someone was keeping their eyes on the road, Jules thought. That was something, anyway! "Just be careful," the teacher was cautioning. "After all, the roads are pretty slick, and we wouldn't want to—"

Just then the bus revved its engine, making the tires spin even faster. Jules heard a strange wet sound, almost like the noise a can of soda made when you slid it down the table. The bus slid sideways—not because Bud had turned the wheel, and not headfirst, but the entire bus essentially shimmied to the right.

"Hydroplane!" Mr. Enright finished, clutching the bar in front of his seat with both hands. "Don't panic, anyone! The bus is programmed to handle this!"

Indeed, it looked to Jules like Bud, at least, wasn't even a little bit worried. He still sat there in the driver's seat, smiling and chattering away like there was nothing wrong. Meanwhile, the bus continued to slide forward and to the right. The curb was coming up fast along that side!

But just when Jules thought the bus would surely run into the curb, jump it, and drive up onto the sidewalk, she saw the steering wheel turn slightly. Not a hard spin like when turning that corner, but rather a gentle pull down and to the left. Apparently that was just enough, because the bus corrected its angle, straightening out and flying down the road as if nothing had happened. There was a faint shudder as the tires gripped the road again, and Jules could feel them picking up speed again.

"And we're out!" Mr. Enright announced. "Can anyone tell me what just happened?" Leave it to him to turn what was almost a terrible accident into a lesson on the fly!

Jules had half expected Christopher to raise his hand first, but instead it was Tracey. That made sense, though, since Tracey was definitely the most car-obsessed of them all. "We hydroplaned," she answered. "That's when a car's tires lose their grip on the road and slide across a thin sheet of water instead."

"Very good," their teacher said. "And absolutely right. The bus spun its tires too fast for this weather, and particularly this amount of rainfall. The tires were moving too quickly to hold onto the pavement, especially in weather like this, where the road is slick with water. That water got between our tires and the road in a layer, like putting a sheet of glass between your hand and the apple you're trying to grab—doesn't look like much, but you can't get through it. In this case, we couldn't get back on solid ground again."

Now Christopher raised his hand, but with a question rather than an answer. "So if you're hydroplaning, what do you do?" he asked. Jules was impressed—she'd originally thought Christopher was just your standard overachieving super-student, willing to go to any lengths to get a good grade, but if that was the case, would he really have admitted he didn't already know something? Anything? Instead, he'd asked a good, practical question.

Mr. Enright seemed to think so as well. "Good question!" he said. "Anybody know the answer?" When no one, not even Tracey, replied after a full minute, he continued with a new question of his own. "Did anyone see how the bus handled it?" he asked.

Jules was one of only two people to raise their hands; the other person was Malik. But Mr. Enright gestured toward Jules. "It turned its wheel," she answered quickly. "But only once. And not all that much."

"That's right," their teacher said. "When you're driving and you suddenly lose control of your car, your first instinct is to slam on the brakes. But that's actually a terrible thing to do here. If you did that, your tires would lock up completely, and you'd really have no way of getting everything back under control. The other thing you absolutely shouldn't do is yank hard on the wheel to get back on track. The problem is, by moving the wheel that fast, you run the risk of locking things up again, or keeping them locked, or whatever. So instead, you turn the wheel, but only a little bit. You take your foot off both the gas and the brake. You let the flow of the water direct where you will go, at least physically. Steer into it rather than away from it, and that will let you keep some control. For example, if you were on a giant cruise ship and it was about to crash into the docks and kill hundreds of people, that's a problem. But you can't turn the ship around; there isn't time for that. And you can't bring it to a complete stop—there's not enough time and not enough space, either. But you may be able to shift the wheel just enough to send the boat heading toward the easternmost corner of the docks, which doesn't currently have any other ships and wouldn't have that many people around. You can't stop the ship from crashing, but you can take control of that crash and thus minimize the damage. That's what the bus did."

"So you steer into it?" Ilyana asked. "Instead of trying to break away?" She considered that. "Okay, I can see that working."

"What else would help?" Mr. Enright continued. "Anybody know?"

After a second, Malik raised his hand. "You could slow down," he suggested, darting a quick, nervous glance toward Bud. But their monkey driver seemed oblivious, focusing once again on the streets all around them and on the type of people who frequented such places. "That way, with the tires spinning more slowly, they'd have a better chance of gripping the road so you could drive normally again."

Their teacher nodded. "Exactly right! There are ways to avoid hydroplaning and ways to manage if you do wind up hydroplaning. The most important thing is to stay calm, don't panic, and don't overreact by spinning the wheel or stomping the brakes. Take your foot off the gas, don't touch the brakes, and steer into the slide so you can control the car and bring it back out safely."

"Is that more STEM use?" Jules asked.

Mr. Enright beamed at her. "It certainly is! It's applying science—in this case, physics— and mechanical engineering to the problem of hydroplaning."

Mechanical engineering is a branch of engineering focused specifically on designing and using machinery.

Jules sank back into her seat. She was pleased with herself for having recognized that. And thinking about it had taken her mind off the near-accident. Even though she was thinking about it again now, the initial panic had passed, so now it felt like just an interesting thing that had happened to them, rather than something to get upset about. After all, Bud had handled it properly. Or the bus had. Whatever.

Settling down a little, Jules looked around her. The other kids also seemed to be relaxing more, now that the initial shock of having a chimpanzee chauffeur—or a self-driving school bus!—and the stress of the hydroplaning incident were wearing off. Randall looked downright excited, like being tossed around on a runaway bus in pouring rain was the best thing to ever happen to him. Mr. Enright, of course, hadn't looked worried at all. But then again, he was presumably the one who'd gotten them a bus that drove itself in the first place!

Now that she wasn't worrying about their driver, Jules was able to concentrate a little more on their surroundings and their destination. The bus had made another turn, though not as sharply this time, and then gone up a ramp and was now zooming along the freeway. Which meant that, wherever they were going, it wasn't close by.

Another car drove past on their left side. As Jules

looked on, she saw the older woman in the car's
passenger seat glance over at the bus, see Bud in the
driver's seat, and do a double-take. Bud had spotted
her as well and beamed, showing all his teeth. The
woman looked like she was going to faint, and Jules
had to laugh as the car pulled away from them. That
lady would certainly have a story to tell!

Jules glanced at her watch. Normally they'd be
almost done with class, and school, by this point. But
evidently that schedule didn't apply to field trips with

Mr. Enright! Fortunately, basketball practice didn't start until next week. And since the principal had obviously been standing right there when they'd left, presumably she would call everyone's parents and let them know why their kids weren't home at the end of the day.

She wondered what any of her classmates would do if they normally took the regular, old-fashioned, driven-by-a-normal-person school bus. It'd be long gone by the time they got back from whatever this was. What if their parents couldn't come pick them up? Would Mr. Enright have the bus drive each of them back? Maybe with Bud still occupying the driver's seat? Jules couldn't help but laugh at the image of the chimp pulling up at each kid's house and letting them out, and especially at the expressions of their parents as they saw who appeared to be driving!

After a second, Jules decided to stop worrying about things like that. Mr. Enright seemed to have a plan, and he was their teacher. She'd just have to trust that he knew what he was doing. She forced herself to stare out the window—at the trees and houses and other cars whizzing past, many of them only just visible as hazy outlines through the downpour. Not a lot of people could say they'd been driven around by a driverless bus, or by a monkey—she might as well enjoy it!

CHAPTER 10

MEETING OF THE MINDS

A few minutes later, the bus pulled to a stop. Peering through the front window, Malik saw that they had reached a street corner, and that just past them was a row of barricades. Where were they going?

"We'll have to walk from here," Mr. Enright announced. He rose from his seat, grabbed a large duffel bag that had been on the seat across from him, and walked down the aisle, handing out brightly colored items from the bag. They turned out to be rain slickers and rain boots. "You'll want to put these on," he said as he offered a set to Malik.

"I had rain gear back in my locker," Malik complained, studying the garish green gear in his hands. "You know, stuff that actually fit me? And didn't make me look like the world's biggest avocado?" From the front, Bud chittered, and Malik shot a glare his way.

"Perhaps, but these are a lot more durable," their teacher replied, heading back to his own seat now

95

that each student—and Randall—had a set. He sat and hauled on a pair of boots himself. They were a lot sturdier than his own galoshes, Malik realized, and they rose well past the knee. The rain slicker was tough as well, and hooded, and it fell to a little below the knee. Once they were all suited up, only their faces and hands were exposed. Malik had to admit that this was a lot better than his own set, at least in terms of facing the thunderstorm outside.

"Everybody ready?" Mr. Enright asked a minute later. There were nods all around, and he turned toward the door.

"On your feet!" Randall bellowed. "Prepare to disembark, on my mark!" Somehow he didn't look ridiculous in his bright red rain gear. Just prepared.

"Why can't we drive to wherever it is we're going?" Ilyana asked as they all climbed off the bus and into brisk winds and pelting rain. "I mean, I know there're those barriers up ahead, but couldn't we just move them out of the way and then put them back in place behind us?" She was already shivering, even though it wasn't all that cold. This was California, after all.

"We could," Mr. Enright answered, closing the bus door behind him once everyone was out, "but it's much too dangerous. We're entering the flood area, and it's not safe to drive through that." He paused and glanced back at his students. "Anyone want to guess why?"

"Because you can't see where you're going with all this rain?" Malik offered.

"Because of the whole hydroplaning thing?" Tracey added.

"Because if you're caught in a flash flood, it could carry you off, car and all," Christopher said. The others stopped and stared at him, and he shrugged. "I saw a report on the news once where that happened."

"Christopher nailed it," their teacher confirmed. "The biggest danger involving vehicles in a flash flood isn't visibility—often the flooding is caused by rain somewhere nearby, and you can see just fine around you. And hydroplaning is bad, sure. But getting carried away can happen even if you're parked. And it doesn't take a whole lot, either. About two feet of water."

"What? How does that work?" Jules demanded. "A car's, like, five feet high and weighs a couple tons. How can two feet of water mess with it? That shouldn't even be enough to leak inside!"

"It has to do with buoyancy, mostly," Mr. Enright answered. "Most cars only weigh a couple of tons, just like Jules said. That's two to four thousand pounds. A foot of water can reduce a car's displacement— how much water it shoves aside—by around fifteen hundred pounds. So for every foot of water, a car effectively weighs fifteen hundred pounds less. That means that, if the car is stuck in two feet of water, it weighs three thousand pounds less, or a ton and a half. Which means if there's two and a half to three feet of water, there's enough buoyancy to make most cars float. And if they're floating, they can wash away just like a life raft or a canoe, or anything else in the water."

Buoyancy is the ability to float in water or some other liquid.

"Wow, that's seriously dangerous," Ilyana said. She glanced back at the bus they'd left behind. "I guess it is a good thing we're leaving it behind, then."

"Absolutely," Mr. Enright agreed. "Now come on. We've got some people I'd like you to meet."

He led them between the barricades and down the street, leaning into the wind and rain to keep it from blowing him back or knocking him off his feet. The kids fell into line behind him, letting their teacher's taller frame shield them from some of the weather, with Randall marching along in the rear shouting things like "Left, right, left!" and that old song about a woman who "looked good, looked fine." The ground here angled up slightly, which was good because it meant they wouldn't wind up in any deep puddles,

Malik thought. Up ahead, however, the direction changed—evidently they were climbing a very low, very shallow hill, and they were almost to the top, because past that point the ground began to angle back away from them. But right near that top was a large, sturdy-looking white tent, the kind that could fit tables and chairs for a meeting or a picnic and that had big, thick stakes holding the ropes taut on every side.

Several people were walking around outside in the rain, all wearing gear similar to what Mr. Enright and the kids had on, but he ignored them all in order to march straight to the tent, where he lifted a flap and ushered the kids inside.

"Ah, there you are, Todd," a short, stocky man with thinning, graying hair called out from a large table in the center of the tent space. "I was starting to worry that you wouldn't be able to get to us in all this."

"This? Ha!" Mr. Enright responded, shaking rain off his slicker. "After that one time in Jakarta, this is nothing! At least I don't have to deal with elephants and monkeys this time! And of course that guerilla leader." He seemed to forcibly stop himself from saying anything else—Randall in particular was leaning in, clearly hanging on their teacher's every word—and instead turned to Malik and the others.

"Class, this is Dr. Henry Lang, a hydrometeorologist the mayor has put in charge of the flash food efforts. Hank, this is STEM Class One."

A **hydrometeorologist** is a scientist who studies water in the atmosphere, particularly in terms of precipitation (such as rain or snow) and its effects upon society. It is a branch of meteorology.

"Pleasure to meet you all," Dr. Lang told them. "Any friend of Todd's is a friend of mine, and I think it's great what he's doing with your class. You're really lucky."

He isn't the first person to say that to us, Malik thought. It was always nice to hear, though. Especially since Dr. Lang clearly had nothing to gain by complimenting their class or their teacher. Malik did have to wonder, though, how the two men knew each other. And what had that been about Jakarta? And elephants?

"Well, welcome to Command Central," Dr. Lang continued, sweeping one arm around to indicate the entire tent and everyone in it. Malik counted five separate tables, each with its own collection of computers, monitors, maps, models, and people. "From here we monitor the entire situation and weigh all of our options."

"A command post," Randall commented. He'd

settled into his usual "at ease" posture and was surveying the room. "Excellent!"

"What sort of options are we talking about?" Tracey called out from the back of the group. "What is the situation? And who's 'we,' anyway?"

Their host chose to answer the last question first. "'We' is the Southern California Flood Crisis Management Team," he replied proudly. "We're a collection of scientists and engineers the cities in this region can call whenever there's a problem involving water levels and flooding—like the torrential rain we've been experiencing the last few days, and the flooding that's caused in several low-lying areas, including this particular neighborhood." He studied the five kids. "Any of you want to guess just how much rainfall we've had since all this started?"

Malik thought back to the first day of school, when they'd predicted ten to twelve inches. And that had been three days ago, with the storm holding steady for most of that time. "Forty-eight inches?" he offered.

"Very good!" Dr. Lang replied, giving Malik a nod. "Official estimate is fifty-one, so you're right on target!" He let his gaze encompass the whole class again. "That's over four feet," he pointed out, and held his hand up to his stomach. "Or right around here. So if the water has pooled anywhere, I'd be in it above my waist. Now imagine all that water collecting throughout the city. Most houses have ceilings that are seven to eight feet high, so the water would fill the first floor halfway. When you think of it like that, you can see why there's been a problem with flooding."

"Okay, sure," Jules agreed. "It's definitely a problem. So what're you doing about it?"

Dr. Lang fixed her with a sharp eye. "An excellent question," he agreed. "What do you think we should be doing?" He glanced over at the other kids, too. "This neighborhood's flooded. How can we fix that?"

Malik stared at the man and knew his classmates were doing the same. What was up with this guy? He was the expert! Why was he asking them what to do?

CHAPTER 11

CRACKING DOWN

"Is this some kind of joke?" Jules demanded. "How should we know? We're just kids!"

"Are you really?" Dr. Lang asked her. "I doubt that." He pointed at her. "For example, I recognize you—you led your basketball team to regionals last year, didn't you?" Jules flushed slightly, both embarrassed and pleased at being recognized. "But that means you're not just a kid," the scientist continued. "You *are* a kid, but you're also an athlete." He scanned the young faces before him. "Each of you is something, or several somethings, already. Not everything you know or can do will apply here, but some of it will. And some of it may even let you think of solutions that never would have occurred to us, because we're approaching it from a different perspective." He looked at each of them. "That's why I asked you what you thought we should do."

Ilyana nodded. "I get it," she said shyly. "No two artists see art the same way, and if you ask one for

103

suggestions, she might tell you something you'd never have thought of on your own, because her ideas about art are different from yours. Not better or worse, just different."

"Exactly," Dr. Lang agreed. "So, tell me your ideas. What do we do next?"

"We've got to stop the water, duh," Malik replied. "If you don't do that, it's just gonna get worse."

"Okay, sure, but that's not easy," Dr. Lang told them. "This area's a floodplain. That means it's a broad, flat stretch of land that's lower than the land on either side and that's near a river or lake. Floodplains flood more easily than anywhere else because they're right next to water and they're lower down, so once the water spills over it pools there."

"Why would anybody want to live on a floodplain, then?" Tracey asked. She shrugged. "Seems like a dumb idea to me."

This time it was Mr. Enright who answered. "Unfortunately, floodplains make very desirable residential neighborhoods," their teacher said, straightening from where he'd been leaning against the map table. "They're wide and flat—great for building—and the soil is thick and rich—perfect for planting. And some floodplains formed centuries ago and don't pose much risk anymore, thanks to the nearby waterways having moved or dried up over the years. Then there are ones like this one that still flood regularly, but people don't always think about that when looking for a house." His lips twitched in a small smirk. "And it's not exactly high on the list of things realtors want to tell potential home buyers."

"*Can* we stop the water somehow?" Jules asked. "I know we can't stop it from raining ever, but maybe there's some way to stop the water from getting down here?"

"We can sandbag along the bank," a woman who'd been sitting back near the far corner of the tent offered. She rose and approached the group. She wasn't very tall and had short, close-cropped blond hair and a serious face, but she was smiling and her eyes were bright with interest. "Tanya Nellis," she introduced herself. "I'm a civil engineer with the city."

A **civil engineer** designs public works, meaning construction that is used by the general public, like roads and bridges.

"Sandbagging—that's when you pile up large burlap sacks filled with sand to block water," Christopher offered. He looked very pleased with himself for having the answer so quickly.

"That's right," Tanya told him. "We can pile them up around the edges of the floodplain to try to keep water from spilling down here. That's only a temporary solution, though—eventually the water does seep through, and the bags will disintegrate over time. We can build a permanent barrier, like some sort of low seawall, most likely out of concrete, but that takes time to construct, and if the waves get high enough they'll still come over that."

"Too bad we can't just install a big drain at the bottom," Jules offered. "Then we wouldn't have to worry about it."

"Actually, that's not as crazy as it sounds," another man who'd been sitting back replied. He was tall and thin, with dark skin and even darker hair in a close halo around his head. "Mike Dunham," he told them. "I'm a geologist." He turned toward the area map and gestured for the students to all gather around as well. "There are several deep fissures that've developed near the edges of the floodplain," he explained, pointing to a few spots where the elevation markings changed drastically. "If we can enlarge some of those, the water could drain off all on its own."

A **geologist** studies rocks and soil, particularly as a way of learning how the Earth was formed.

"What do you mean, a fissure?" Jules asked. She was surprised but thrilled that her off-the-cuff remark might actually be important.

"Oh, sorry. Fissures are narrow, deep cracks in the

ground," Dr. Lang said. "The edges of the floodplain are riddled with them."

"It's because of the tectonic instability in the region as a whole," Mike continued, then chuckled at the looks of confusion on most of the kids' faces. "Sorry, fell into geek-speak there for a second. California has a lot of earthquakes, which means the ground here is frequently shifting around. That causes cracks, like these fissures." His eyes lit up. "Wanna see one?"

Tectonics refers to the Earth's upper layer, its crust, and the way that layer forms and shifts.

There was an immediate chorus of "yes" and "absolutely!" and "oh, heck yeah," and so on, and the geologist chuckled as he led them out of the tent and along the small rise it stood upon. "Look over here," he called over his shoulder, stopping perhaps thirty yards from the tent and gesturing ahead of him. The kids quickly gathered around him. "Voila!"

Sure enough, there in the ground some forty feet away was a deep cleft, as if some giant had brought an axe down and split the ground in two. The fissure was only one or two feet wide and perhaps five feet long, tapering out of existence at both ends, but inside it was pitch black, with no hint of a bottom.

"Man, that is so sick!" Malik exclaimed. He

whipped out his phone. "I've gotta get a picture of this!"

"Careful," Mr. Enright warned—he had followed the little group out of the tent. "Don't get too close."

"Or what?" Malik retorted, snapping pictures. "It's gonna swallow me up? Please!"

"You heard the man!" Randall snapped, crossing muscular arms over his chest. "Get back here on the double!"

"Yeah, whatever," Malik replied. Annoyed at the aide's attitude, he slowly walked forward until he was right next to the fissure. Then, with a deliberate smirk, he lifted one foot, swung it outward, and brought it back down—on the fissure's other side.

"Check it out!" Malik declared, snapping a selfie. "I'm like a human bridge!"

"Um, I really wouldn't recommend that," Christopher warned quietly. "Statistically, there is—"

"Chill, dude," Malik interrupted. "It's all good. See?" He crouched to get a better shot of himself and the fissure together.

Which was when they heard the loud creak, like a stubborn old door being forced open.

A creak that was coming from right below Malik.

"Get back here!" Mr. Enright insisted. Malik shrugged and straightened up, which was exactly when the rain-soaked edges of the fissure crumbled away,

dirt and rock disappearing down into that dark space as it widened dramatically—directly beneath Malik's feet.

"Ahh!" The lanky preteen cried out as he flailed for solid ground. "I'm sorry, I'll take the photos back down!"

Jules had reacted the second they heard the fissure crack. She lunged forward, pushing past the other students to stand right before the fissure. "Grab my hand!" she instructed, reaching out for Malik. He shot out his right hand, and Jules grabbed it firmly, her fingers almost wrapping around his forearm. But even with her muscle she couldn't hold him one-handed, and her feet slid across the ground as his weight pulled her closer to the edge, the two of them teetering like a deadly seesaw. "The other one!" she insisted through clenched teeth.

"But, my phone!" Malik shouted.

"It's the phone or you!" she replied.

More of the ground disappeared, and Malik gulped. His hand opened, the phone falling away and vanishing into the fissure as he grabbed Jules's other hand with his. With both hands locked, she was able to get better leverage, and a good hard tug sent Malik flying toward her, Jules herself falling back at the same time. She landed on her butt several feet from the fissure's new edge, Malik sprawling half across her.

"Get off me!" she shouted, shoving him aside and rising to her feet in a single smooth motion.

"Sorry," Malik mumbled. He sat up and turned to stare back at the fissure that had nearly claimed his life. "Uh, thanks."

There hadn't been time, or space, for anyone else to push up close to Malik or Jules before, especially with the fissure expanding. But now Mr. Enright was able to reach them, Randall right behind him. "Are you both okay?" their teacher asked, crouching down beside Malik.

"Fine," Jules reported. She stalked off back toward the others.

Mike joined them. He looked embarrassed. "That shouldn't have happened," he explained quietly, running a hand over his face. "There must be some other cracks around, small ones, and the water got in there and split the rock face. I'm really sorry."

"Eh, it's all good," Malik answered, apparently already over his near-disaster. "I'm still here, right?" He pulled himself up and tried brushing off all the dirt and mud that had now soaked into his outfit despite the heavy slicker. "Man, good thing I can't take a selfie right now—I'm a mess!" he joked.

Mr. Enright shook his head. "Let's get back to the tent," he suggested, standing himself. "Oh, and Malik?"

"Yes, sir?"

The teacher sighed. "Let's not mention this to Dr. Pillai, okay?" He glanced at Randall, who was once again right behind him. "That goes for you as well, Randall."

"Sir, yes sir," Randall replied sharply. "Not a word, sir! Operational silence!"

Malik agreed as well and let himself be led back to safety. The rest of the class, which had stayed well back of the drama, watched for a second before following them back inside.

"Dude," Ilyana whispered to Jules as they waited their turn. "This is so much better than some old museum tour!"

Despite being annoyed at Malik for his crazy stunt, and hurting a bit from yanking him back from certain death, Jules grinned back at her. "I know, right?" Giggling, the two girls ducked back into the tent.

CHAPTER 12
PROBLEMS AND SOLUTIONS

"Okay, so we could maybe use those fissures to drain off the water," Tracey offered once they were all back inside. She glanced over at Malik. "Provided Malik doesn't plug them all up with his phone—or his butt!"

"Ha ha," Malik replied, trying yet again to brush off some of the muck he'd accumulated outside. He wasn't actually mad at her, though. It was kind of funny! And he thought it was a lot better to laugh at how silly he'd been than to get all upset about how close he'd come to plunging into that hole! "Too bad I can't control where they go, or maybe I would," he joked back.

"That is the biggest problem with trying to use the fissures," Mike agreed. "If we can locate a fissure and figure out where it opens back out, we could try using it, funneling the floodwaters toward it. But most of the time we don't know where those cracks lead. If they pass under an already unstable section of rock, pouring a whole bunch of water down there could destabilize the region further. That's one way you get sinkholes, by washing away the rock and soil beneath the surface so that what looks like solid ground is actually just a thin skin over a hole, like putting plastic wrap over a bowl. Rest something gently on top of that plastic and it's fine, but puncture it and everything goes tumbling down."

"Do you usually get sinkholes like that on floodplains?" Ilyana asked.

The geologist shook his head. "No, floodplains are the lowest land in the region," he answered. "That means they tend to be stable, which is another reason why people like to build on them. Sinkholes are typically at a higher elevation, like along a ridge overlooking a floodplain." He glanced pointedly down at the kids. "Like the one we're on right now."

Oh, great. Malik glanced down at the ground beneath his feet uneasily, worried that it would suddenly collapse beneath him. Hadn't he done this enough already? The others looked equally worried.

"Don't worry," Dr. Lang assured them, glaring at Mike, who just shrugged playfully. "We chose this spot because it's actually a solid spur of rock. No chance of washing away from here!"

"Those homes down there could wash away, though," Christopher commented. He was looking at the map, which showed the neighborhood below this ridge.

"They could," a woman agreed, approaching them. She was tall and pretty—even with her dark hair pulled back in a simple ponytail—and wearing worn jeans and a faded T-shirt, she looked more like a model than what Malik thought of when he pictured a scientist. He was starting to realize there was no "typical" scientist.

"Kelly Dellacoe," she introduced herself. "I'm an architectural engineer. Mike's area is the ground beneath our feet, and Tanya's is the pipes and streets and other city structures. Mine is the buildings themselves and what to do about them."

An **architectural engineer** is an engineer who focuses on the design and construction of buildings.

"Can those homes be saved?" Malik asked. He hated the idea of people losing their homes to the flooding. That would suck!

Fortunately, Kelly was already nodding. "Most of them can," she replied. "Especially if we can act fast. The longer those homes sit in water, the more damaged they get, and the harder it'll be to recover them." She smiled at the students. "You ever see what happens to a piece of wood if you soak it?"

Most of them shook their heads, but not Ilyana. "It gets all soft and warped," she answered. "That happened to a spot on my grandpa's deck last year— some water pooled there and sat for months, and it just fell apart. They had to cut around it and replace the whole section."

"Exactly," Kelly said. "Wood's good and strong and solid—as long as it stays dry. And it can handle a certain amount of water without a problem, especially if you wipe it off afterward. But if it soaks too long, it gets soft and mushy and crumbles away. The same's true of masonite board and plaster, and those three make up the walls of most modern homes."

"What about brick?" Malik asked. "Water doesn't damage that, does it?" His house was brick.

"Bricks can crumble away the same way," the architectural engineer told him, "but it takes a lot more water to do that, and a lot more time. However, bricks are held together by mortar, and that'll disintegrate long before the bricks do, so even though a wall could look solid, a single push—or a stiff wind— can knock it right over."

"So how do we fix that?" Tracey asked.

"We get the water off them," Christopher suggested. He fingered a leather band around his wrist. "Keep any new water back, and dry off the water that's already there."

"Drying them off is exactly right," Kelly confirmed. "We've got some industrial dryers on the way. They're like the world's largest blow-dryers. Once they're here, we'll set them up to dry out the homes before their walls and foundations can collapse."

"How does that work in the rain, though?" Malik wanted to know. "Won't everything just get wet all over again? And what about the dryers themselves? What if they get wet? Won't they short out?"

"They could," Kelly admitted, "Which is why we'll cover them with thick tarps to keep them as dry as possible. They're already built with a lot of shielding, so that'll help too. But you're right, if this rain stops, it'll make our job a whole lot easier."

"So what do you do once you've dried everything out?" Jules asked. "That's not it, right?"

"Not even close," Kelly answered. She held up the biggest marker the kids had ever seen—it was as thick around as a little kid's arm! "Once it's all dry we go in and inspect each house. We use markers like this to circle any problems and danger spots so that we know what needs fixing. Sometimes it's just a matter of replacing a section of wall or floor, like on your grandpa's deck." She pointed to Ilyana. "But other times the water's gotten into the wiring, or it's already weakened floor joists or ceiling supports or something

117

else major. Then we've got our work cut out for us."

Mr. Enright had been listening to the conversation. Now he chimed in. "Of course, even though Kelly and her team will do their best to restore each and every damaged home, that doesn't help much if they just get destroyed again in the next flash flood. So they also do their best to make sure these houses won't be as vulnerable in the future."

"That's right." Kelly studied the kids. "Can anybody guess one way to do that?" Nobody answered. "What's one of the most dangerous things in a house to get wet?" she asked.

"The fuse box!" Tracey replied. Everybody else muttered in agreement. They might not be electricians, but they knew that getting a fuse box wet would be bad. It'd cause everything to short circuit, or something like that!

"Absolutely," Kelly said. "And most fuse boxes are either on the first floor, like in a garage, or in the basement. But if you're on a floodplain, that's a bad idea! So we'll reroute everything in these houses and move their fuse boxes to the second floor, where they're a lot less likely to get wet."

"Is there any way to waterproof the whole house?" Christopher asked. "Wouldn't that keep it safe from flooding?"

Tanya joined them. "There are ways, yes," the

short civil engineer answered. "The most common way is to seal every joint and angle to make sure water can't leak in. Then there are a few compounds you can spray on a surface so water just beads off it—use that on your foundation and the lower portion of your first floor and you'll have eliminated most ways water can get in and start ruining everything." She shook her head. "Nothing's a hundred percent, of course, but the good news is, waterproofing is easy to do and it doesn't hurt anything if it turns out you never need it."

"So first we need to draw the water off of the floodplain," Malik summarized. "Then we need to dry out the houses wherever they got damaged. Then we need to go through and mark wherever the houses took water damage and help repair those places."

"And then we have to move things around and waterproof the outside so that, if it ever rains like this again, all those homes will still be fine," Jules added.

"Yeah, no pressure," Malik joked, and the others laughed. But deep inside, his stomach was in knots. Because there was a *lot* of pressure, actually. It was easy for them to stand up here laughing and joking and coming up with all these crazy plans. But for the people who lived down on that floodplain, these were their homes. Everything they had was in those buildings. A lot of them couldn't afford to have their homes repaired, not if the damage was severe. So it was actually really important that Dr. Lang and Kelly and Mike and Tanya and the others did the best job they possibly could. They had to save as much here as possible, and do it as quickly as possible.

They didn't really have time to babysit a bunch of high school kids.

But Mr. Enright had apparently noticed something in Malik's face, or in his tone, and now the teacher stepped around the others to join Malik by the corner of the map table he'd staked out. "I know this all seems like a lot," Mr. Enright said quietly. "But this is what STEM does—find a problem, then propose and test out various solutions until you find one that works. And right now we need all the solutions we can get." He rested a hand on Malik's shoulder. "It's easy to get overwhelmed by everything that needs doing, especially in a situation like this, where an entire neighborhood is at stake. But if you break everything down into small, manageable goals and have a lot of willing hands and sharp minds to share the load, you'll find it's a lot easier. And you'll get a lot more done." The teacher looked down at him. "Just don't put 'falls into a fissure' on that list, okay?"

Malik laughed. "Yeah, trust me, I won't," he promised. He already felt a little better. After all, these scientists were taking the time to talk with them and were listening seriously to their suggestions. So maybe they really could help. And if they could do anything for all those people and their homes and favorite items and photos and other memories, well, then—Malik took a deep breath and turned back toward the others, forcing himself to join the conversation taking place—that was definitely something they should do.

This was, he had to admit, at least to himself, shaping up to certainly be the most interesting and possibly even the best field trip ever!

CHAPTER 13

DEVISING A PLAN

Another pair joined them, a man and a woman. The man was large and heavyset, with a full reddish-brown beard and thick hair the same shade. Wearing a flannel shirt and jeans, he looked more like a lumberjack than any sort of scientist. Then again, Jules thought, looking over her classmates, who were they to judge?

The woman was more what Jules would have expected from a professional. She was tiny, barely Jules's height, with dark hair pulled back in a sensible bun and dark, alert eyes. A small smile hovered on her lips, like she was thinking of something funny but didn't want to share. Still, somehow Jules could tell the joke wasn't on them—whoever she was, this woman seemed too kind for that.

"Hi, I'm Rachel, Rachel Goldstein," the woman announced, her smile broadening into a friendly welcome. "I'm an ecologist. My job on the team is to minimize the damage the flood—and our efforts—

causes to not only the floodplain and its homes but also to the surrounding area and the environment as a whole."

"And I'm Anthony Lemus," the man added. "I'm a hydrologist." He paused for a second, waiting for the inevitable. Jules decided she wasn't going to oblige, but Ilyana did it for her.

"What's a hydrologist?" she asked. "You study water?"

He laughed, long and loud. He even laughs like a lumberjack, Jules thought. "That's exactly right," he agreed after he'd recovered. "I study water. Specifically, the properties of water, its movement, and the effects on its surroundings."

"So you're less concerned with the houses than with the water flooding them?" Malik asked.

"Sure," Anthony agreed easily. "Plenty of others here to worry about those homes, which is great—I'm not saying those aren't important. But what happens to the water itself? If we drain it all off to bail out those houses, where does it all go?"

"Can we evaporate it? Send it back up into the air?" Ilyana asked.

Evaporation is when a liquid changes to a gas. Most often this is caused by heat, when the liquid in question reaches its boiling point.

The hydrologist frowned through his beard. "That might be possible," he admitted slowly, "if we used some big heaters to boil it back to gaseous form. But that'd just add to the general humidity and increase the chance of more rain, which would put us right back where we started."

"If we pour it into a fissure, it'll flow away

somewhere else," Tracey said, but Anthony shook his head.

"But where?" he asked. "Do you know? No, of course you don't—you can't. Nobody does. We're still trying to map things like that, but they're constantly changing. Is the water going to flow under something and destabilize it? Is it going to come pouring out along a cliff face, directly onto another community? Or a roadway? Or is going to add to an underground river and raise it an inch or two but not have any real impact? That's what we have to find out. Otherwise we could make things worse rather than better."

"Okay, but how do we do that?" Tracey demanded. "How can we figure out where it's going ahead of time?"

Jules thought maybe the bearded scientist would get mad at being interrogated by a high schooler, but instead he looked pleased, like she'd just given him the best birthday present ever.

"We redirect it!" he declared, throwing his arms wide. "That way we know exactly where it's going!"

"And we can send it where it'll do the most good," Rachel added. It was funny that she was so short, she didn't even have to duck to avoid her colleague's arm. "There are places, even in this county, suffering from water shortages."

"Right now?" Jules asked. "Really?"

But Rachel just laughed. "Absolutely," she replied. "Sure, they're getting a ton of rain this week, but they've been bone-dry for months before that, so that's not really enough. And it's uncontrolled—do you know what happens to soil when it hasn't gotten any water in months?"

"It dries out?" Christopher offered.

"Exactly right! And, if there's heavy sunlight, it not only dries out, it bakes! You get mud pies, just like when you were a kid." She chuckled, and Jules could totally picture the tiny ecologist in pigtails playing in the mud. "And what happened when you poured water onto a baked mud pie?"

This one Jules remembered, though more from watching little cousins do it at a family gathering last year. "It cracks and crumbles away," she said.

Rachel beamed at her. "Yes! So we can't count on this flood helping those areas—in a lot of cases, it's actually going to wash away the usable soil, so when the rain stops, they'll be in even worse shape than they would've been without it. That means that if we want all this water to go to the best use, we have to store it somewhere and dole it out as we need it, instead of just dumping it on them."

"So we build storage units," Ilyana said. "We funnel the water into them, and then we figure out where to send them."

Malik perked up. "Maybe we can somehow put containers in the fissures," he suggested, "and that way the water'll pour in all on its own." He laughed. "Just as long as I'm not in there with them." Jules was glad to see he'd gotten over any embarrassment from his little near-disaster earlier. She felt a little bad for snapping at him too. She'd just been running on adrenaline at the time, and that always made her short-tempered.

"That's actually a great idea," Anthony enthused. The other scientists had gathered around to listen in on the conversation, and several of them were nodding as well. "We could set up some kind of drain system, maybe, to catch the water and then run it off somewhere." Some of them started talking together, bouncing ideas around about how this could work, and Jules saw that Malik was practically beaming with pride. She couldn't blame him, either. He'd offered an idea, and here was a group of grown-up scientists getting all excited about it and talking about how to make it a reality. How cool was that?

The other kids got caught up in it as well. "We could map out which parts of the county need water the most," Tracey said, "so that we could prioritize where to send the water first."

"That's great!" Rachel agreed. "I've got some of that information already, but I haven't looked at it like that before. It's more of an overview of the county, but you're right—if we use this as the central point and fan out from here, we could really see where the water should go first, and what's easiest to reach." She pulled out her phone and started typing on it furiously.

"What about using it for drinking water?" Ilyana asked. "Is that a thing?"

"Oh, it's definitely a thing," Anthony replied. "And you're right, that's an excellent idea. We could collect some of the water and place it in cisterns equipped with water filtration units, like smaller versions of the big water towers you see outside small towns and even atop some apartment buildings. Then the houses could use that water instead of piping it in from the city. And if we set up the filtration systems properly, any new rainfall would add to their cisterns, refilling them so they could continue to draw water that way. It's a great way to make sure it gets used, and it doesn't even require us to move it away from here, which would make things a lot easier."

A **cistern** is a tank or reservoir used for storing water.

"I can help set those up," Rachel offered. She studied the kids with a smile. "And I'd be happy to have some help from the more mechanically minded among you." Tracey all but jumped to her feet at that, and Rachel's grin widened. "Looks like I've got a volunteer."

Jules turned to Mr. Enright, who'd been watching all of this from the side. "Is that really something we can do?" she asked him. She pulled out her phone and glanced at the screen. "Class is already over, right? How long is this field trip? Not that I'm complaining," she added hastily. "I was just curious how much time we really had, and if we could actually start helping with some of this stuff."

Her teacher studied her for a second. "Do you want to help?" he asked finally.

"Definitely!" Her classmates all chimed in their interest as well.

The smile that got them was the same one Mr. Enright had displayed after they'd fixed the leaky pipe back at school. "Brilliant!" he told them. He glanced lazily at his watch. "Well, I suppose we can stay a little longer, in that case." But the way he said it, Jules could tell he was happy about the idea too, and she suspected he'd already planned for them be here for a while longer. She didn't care, though. She was enjoying herself, and she knew the others were too. They were getting to contribute real ideas on how to help, and now they might actually get to help make those a reality too!

How epic was that?

CHAPTER 14

OPENING DOORS

Just then, Bud came hurrying back into the tent.
Yet again, Malik hadn't seen the chimp go and
was surprised when he returned. How did somebody
that hairy and chattery move so quietly? Bud went
directly to Mr. Enright, tugged on the teacher's sleeve
to get his attention, and then chittered something and
gestured toward the tent entrance.

"Oh?" Yet again their teacher acted as if he
understood the chimp's weird vocalizations completely.
"Let's see." The two of them retraced Bud's steps—
it was really funny seeing their tall teacher walking
beside the short chimp—and pulled the flap aside to
peer out. "Excellent news, everyone!" Mr. Enright
called back over his shoulder. "The rain has stopped!"

The kids immediately rushed over to crowd around
him, staring outside. Sure enough, nothing was coming
down right now, and Malik squinted. Was that a
bit of blue showing off in the distance? Maybe the
weather was finally clearing up!

"Good timing," Tanya said as she joined them. She held up her phone. "Because I just got a text—the pumps are here!"

"What pumps?" Tracey asked.

"We've got some massive, heavy-duty pumps," she explained, "for exactly this sort of situation. They'll pump the water out from the houses themselves first, and then from the streets around them, so that we can go in, open the windows, set up the dryers, and start getting everything aired out and dried up. That's the first step."

"And we've got containers en route too," Rachel added, "so the water we pump out can be stored and then carted off to places where we can use it." She held up a pad of paper. "I've already started making a list!"

"But for now we're setting up a temporary reservoir made out of sandbags," Anthony said. "Otherwise, we'd have to wait on those containers before we can start work. And the sooner we get that water out of there, the better!"

Jules asked the question that had been on the tip of Malik's tongue as well. "What can we do to help?" Looking at his other classmates, Malik could see they all felt the same way. They wanted to do more than just ask questions and make suggestions!

Mr. Enright glanced over at Dr. Lang and the other scientists. "Perhaps they could be put to work opening windows and doors, pulling curtains out of the way—that sort of thing?" he suggested.

Tracey looked a little disappointed at not being able to help Rachel with the containers, but this was a more urgent need, so she nodded along with the rest of the kids at this suggestion.

"That'd be great," Dr. Lang agreed. "We need all the airways open and unobstructed so the pumps and dryers can be more effective. If you all go in together, you should be fine—just be careful where you step, because things are going to be slippery from all that water. And don't step anywhere you can't see the bottom, in case something's collapsed underneath."

"Randall," Mr. Enright added, turning to his aide. "Can you go with them and make sure they stay safe? I'm going to coordinate a bit more with Dr. Lang and the others up here."

Randall saluted. "Infiltrate a location, secure it, and clear obstructions," he recited. "Roger that!" The teacher's aide turned to Malik and the others. "All right, squad, fall in and move out!"

"Which is it?" Malik replied, irritated by the way the college boy liked to order them around. "Do we fall in, or do we move out? And what're we falling into? Or moving out of?"

His classmates laughed, but Randall scowled at

him. "No insubordination!" he yelled right in Malik's face.

"Malik," Mr. Enright warned, "I know Randall's a bit . . . enthusiastic, but let's all work together on this, shall we? He's also old enough to qualify as an adult, which means I can let all of you go down there together without needing to wait for one of the scientists here to be free to accompany you—but only if I can trust you to function as a unit." It was a mild rebuke, but it still stung, and Malik hung his head.

"Yes, sir," he agreed. Without another word, he slid into place between Christopher and Ilyana.

"I thought it was funny," Ilyana whispered, leaning forward to talk to him. "And he really needs to stop ordering us around."

That made Malik feel a little better, but he still resolved not to let the aide's attitude get to him so much.

With Randall in the lead, the kids exited the tent and started making their way down the slope toward the houses. All around them, Dr. Lang's team scurried about like busy ants, carrying hoses and pipes and tools. Even though the rain had stopped and the sky had cleared a little, it was still overcast, and the ground was muddy and soaked, so they all had to be really careful not to slip and fall. Malik was definitely glad for the heavy rain gear Mr. Enright had provided—the rain boots had thick treads that helped him keep his footing, and the few times he did slide a little, the rain slicker took the brunt of the mud and water.

It took them more than ten minutes to make it all the way down onto the floodplain, and although they all slipped and slid a little, nobody completely wiped out, which was good. It was a relief to put their feet back on solid, stable, level ground again, though, even if it was still in water up to their knees. Then, keeping to the sidewalks, Randall led them to the nearest house.

"First location," he announced, studying the class. "Remember your orders—we enter, we secure it, we remove obstructions, and we exit. No side missions!"

"What's he think, we're gonna go snooping around in people's homes?" Jules muttered. "We're here to help!"

"I think he just enjoys tossing in as many military terms as he can," Tracey replied just as quietly. "Makes him feel all official and stuff."

Still, that was what Dr. Lang had told them to do, so it didn't even matter that Randall was repeating it in his own unique fashion. The kids knew what they were here for, and they were eager to get to it.

"Deploy!" Randall shouted, leading the way to the front door. It wasn't locked, but the water pressing against it had bowed it in its frame, making it difficult to budge. It wound up taking Randall, Jules, and Tracey to force it open. Malik wanted to help, but honestly he was too skinny to add much muscle, and there wasn't room for more than three by the door, so he hung back with Christopher and Ilyana.

When the three were finally able to push the door in a few inches, a wave of water crashed through, as high as their chests and powerful enough to almost knock them from their feet. Malik and the others rushed forward, helping to prop their friends up. It would suck to get overwhelmed like that, and even though the pumps were already beginning to switch on, there was still plenty of standing water—he remembered Mr. Enright's warning about how little it took to carry off an entire car and shuddered. No way that was happening to any of them!

The wave washed through as quickly as it had hit, the water level beyond the door dropping to only a few feet, and now they were able to shove the door the rest of the way open. "The house is a little higher than the ground around it," Christopher pointed out, "so the door was the only thing keeping all that water from flowing downhill."

"Makes our job easier," Malik agreed. "If it drains on its own, they may not even need the pumps in here, just the dryers." They all headed indoors, stepping carefully.

Once inside, the kids split into teams. Malik and Christopher started in the living room, which was to the right. Tracey and Jules headed to the left, where it looked like there might be an office or a guest room. Poor Ilyana got stuck with Randall, who ordered her to accompany him further back, where the kitchen and dining room presumably were. Well, better her than me, Malik thought as he went to the living room's wide bay windows and started opening them. Right beside him, Christopher was already raising the blinds and tying back the curtains.

"Good in here," he announced once they'd finished both those windows and the single, smaller side window. Christopher agreed, and together they headed back to look for the rest of their class.

"All set in the office," Jules declared as they met up in the hall. They found Ilyana and Randall just tying off the last curtain in the dining room, and together the whole class moved into the kitchen. There was a narrow window over the sink there, but the back corner of the room was a breakfast nook with wraparound windows, and all of those needed to be opened and cleared as well. Even so, it didn't look like it would take too long.

"What about the upstairs?" Malik asked as he wrestled with one of the windows. "Do we need to open things up there as well?"

"We should," Jules replied. "Just in case. It can't hurt, right?"

"Hot air rises," Ilyana pointed out. "So if they turn the heaters on down here, all that heat'll rise to the second floor, and then it can escape out the windows up there. Otherwise it could overheat things up there and cause more damage."

That was a good point, and they all agreed to head upstairs once they were done in here. But when Malik finally got the stubborn window free, and shoved it up as far as it would go, he paused.

"Does anybody else hear that?" he asked. There was a steady hum of machinery, which he guessed was the pumps or the dryers or both. And he could hear people moving around and shouting. But beyond that was something else. Something loud and rapid and heavy. It sounded like . . .

It sounded, he realized, like a raging river he'd seen once on a family fishing trip.

And it was getting louder!

CHAPTER 15

UNDER WATER

Jules had heard the water as well and peered out through the breakfast nook's windows. Once her eyes were able to focus, however, she almost wished she hadn't.

Because what she saw was what looked like an entire wall of water, and it was heading their way!

"It's the flood!" she shouted, and the other kids quickly crowded around her to look as well. "It's coming right for us!"

"The reservoir!" Christopher declared. "They were making it out of sandbags. It must not've been strong enough to hold back all the water!"

Which meant, Jules realized, that all the water the crisis team had just pumped out of this valley was now rushing right back in again.

And this house was directly in its path!

"Evac on the double!" Randall announced, grabbing the back door and hauling it open. "Let's move out, team!"

Everyone jumped. Then most of them automatically started after Randall, following the person who sounded like he knew what he was doing. Surprisingly, it was Ilyana who stood her ground. "No!" she shouted back. "We can't! There's too much water, and it's coming too fast! We'll all get swept away! We'll drown, right there in the street!"

What she said made sense. Jules thought about Mr. Enright's impromptu lesson about cars and floodwaters. If it only took two feet of water to carry off a car, they could be in trouble in just a few inches! And there was a lot more than that heading at them!

Randall clearly didn't agree, however. "We're wasting time chit-chatting!" he hollered. "If we're going, we've got to go now! So you're either with me or you're not!" And he lunged through the door and dove directly into the rushing water.

Nobody followed him. Tracey looked like she wanted to grab the teacher's aide and yank him back in, but it was clearly too late for that. Instead, she jumped back and slammed the door behind him, then latched it for good measure. "That's not going to hold," she warned quietly.

"He's crazy!" Malik shouted, still staring at the door. But then he added, "We've got to go after him!"

"And do what?" Jules asked him. "Get swept away right along with him?" She shook her head. "He made his choice, right? We made ours. Done is done."

"Besides, he might be okay," Ilyana offered quietly. "He's a SEAL, isn't he?"

"Well, he sure wanted to be," Malik muttered. But he sounded more sad than bitter.

For a second they all stood there, thinking about the strange aide who'd only been with them for two days and who hadn't exactly been their favorite person but had still been one of them. Sort of. And who was now gone. Maybe for good. But certainly gone somewhere they couldn't follow.

As if to punctuate that point, the kitchen door began to creak. And bow inward. Water was flowing in beneath it and around the edges, and the hinges and lock protested louder and louder with each passing second.

"We need to get to higher ground," Christopher suggested, already backing away. "Second floor, now!"

Nobody argued. Seconds later, the kitchen door burst inward, but by then they were already out of the room and heading down the hall for the stairs. Christopher was in the lead, with Malik right behind him, then Ilyana and Jules, with Tracey bringing up the rear.

Jules had only just set foot on the bottom step when the flood arrived.

With a noise like thunder, it slammed into the front

door, crashing through with such force that the door actually flew off its hinges and careened into the hall, narrowly missing her head before it fell back and was swept away. Jules clung to the banister as the water swirled around her, trying to pull her free and cart her off along with that door.

And Tracey gave a yelp as she went under completely.

Jules didn't even stop to think. She dove after her friend—one hand still wrapped around the banister, the other groping blindly.

There! She touched something like flesh, and something like fabric. That had to be her!

Unable to see, or to breathe, Jules just clamped onto whatever it was as hard as she could and then hauled herself back up onto the steps, trying to take her new prize with her. Whatever it was, it was heavy, and her muscles burned as she tried to pull it free of the water. The current was strong, and getting stronger as the water rose higher and higher, and Jules could feel her grip starting to slip—until another set of hands latched on as well, right above hers.

Jules glanced up to see Malik there beside her, pulling for all he was worth. Christopher had an arm around him, and the other laced through the banister rails, and Ilyana was reaching for Jules to anchor her in the same way.

Now that she didn't have to worry about getting sucked into the water herself, Jules was able to give Tracey—it was clearly her friend that she'd grabbed, she saw now—her full attention. And all her strength. With Malik's help, Jules was able to pull Tracey up onto the steps, where she collapsed beside Jules, soaked head to toe and gasping for air.

"You okay?" Ilyana asked after a second. She'd released Jules and backed up to give her room to breathe as well.

"Oh, aces," Tracey managed, in between gasping and coughing up water. "Just figured I'd get my whole month's showers out of the way all at once, y'know?" Raising herself up on her elbows, she looked at Jules and then at Malik and the others. "Thanks."

Jules smiled, even though she felt like she'd just run a marathon. And gone a few rounds in the ring. With a gorilla. "No worries."

"We need to get higher," Christopher urged, and Jules saw that the water was high enough to lap at her feet already. "Come on." He led them the rest of the way up the stairs.

The second floor had three bedrooms and two bathrooms. Without even stopping to discuss their options, they all headed toward the back of the house, which had the master bedroom and master bathroom.

That was the obvious choice—it was the largest bedroom and could hold the five of them more easily, plus it was farther from the stairs and from the water creeping up them. Malik was the last one through and shut the bedroom door behind him, but they all knew that wouldn't do a whole lot of good. The front door had been solid, and the flood had torn it free like it was paper. The bedroom door was practically a decoration compared to that!

"What're we gonna do if the water reaches this floor?" Malik asked nobody in particular. And nobody had a good answer for that.

"We could try swimming through it once the water's settled a bit," Ilyana offered. "That first big rush was from it all coming back downhill, right? So after the reservoir up there empties, it should stop moving around so much."

But Jules had just noticed an all-too-familiar and right now highly unwelcome sound—a hard, steady pounding on the roof and against the windows. "I don't think that's gonna work," she warned. She went to the nearest window and looked out. Sure enough, the sky had gone slate gray again, and everything was hazy through the deluge that had begun once more. "It's pouring again," she told the others. "So the flooding's only going to get worse."

They all clustered around the window, staring out at the clouds and the storm and the water that was still pouring in around houses and over streets, its surface stippled by the rain from above. "Yeah, no way we're gonna be able to swim through that," Malik agreed. "There's just too much of it, and with the added rain it's gonna keep growing." Plus, from here, the tents back up on the hill looked like they were miles away. Jules knew they weren't—it had only taken them ten minutes to get down here, after all, and that was because they'd been trying not to fall—but the idea of swimming the distance, against a strong current and in punishing rain, especially after she'd already exhausted herself grabbing Tracey, wasn't one she wanted to consider.

"We're going to have to think of something," Christopher replied. "And fast." He pointed back toward the bedroom door, and they all turned—to see water starting to seep in under it, bubbling up through the narrow gap between wood and carpet.

"That means the first floor's completely flooded," Tracey said. She shuddered, and Jules knew her friend was thinking about her recent dip. That and she had to be freezing in her soaked clothes. Jules was shivering from it too, and she was only soaked from the waist up.

"We could try to dive down and swim out that way," Ilyana suggested. "At least if we were under water, the rain wouldn't bother us, and the current might not be as bad underneath."

"Yeah, but what if it is?" Malik countered. "Lots of rivers and oceans have nasty currents hiding deep down where you can't see 'em. And what if we get stuck down there on the first floor? If it's totally filled up, which it must be if the water's already getting up here, we might not have any place where we can come up for air. That happens to divers all the time; they get caught up in a current and then tangled up in coral or seaweed or something under water and can't make their way back to the surface, so they drown." He shook his head. "I think it's just too risky."

Jules found herself agreeing with him. She really didn't like the idea of trying to go back down into that, and the idea of getting stuck under the water was terrifying. But if they didn't do that, what could they do instead?

Whatever it was, they were going to need to figure it out fast, before this room flooded and they were trapped in the water with nowhere else to go!

CHAPTER 16

UP AND OUT

"We need to go higher," Tracey said. "Get on the roof, if we can."

They all looked around. There were the windows, of course, but could they really climb all the way from there up to the roof? In the rain? With the floodwaters right below, waiting to snatch them up if they fell?

Malik closed his eyes and tried to think. He'd glanced up at the house as they'd approached it, hadn't he? What had it looked like? It was two stories, with a sloping roof; he remembered that much. And weren't there—? "Windows," he practically shouted.

Jules raised an eyebrow. "Yeah, right there," she replied, gesturing at the one nearest them. "But that's a hell of a climb, especially in this weather."

"No," Malik told her, "not those windows. There're other windows, higher up. Sticking out of the roof. Two of them." He could picture them in his head, jutting out with little miniature roofs over them as well.

"You mean dormer windows?" Ilyana asked. The others all turned to her, and she shrugged. "I read it in a book," she explained, flicking her hair back over her shoulder. "They'd be in the attic, and Malik's right, we could use those to get right out onto the roof, nice and easy."

"Okay, sure, but how do we get to the attic?" Christopher countered. He scanned the bedroom. "I don't see any stairs or anything."

It was Jules who had the answer to that. "There's a panel in the hall," she said. "I saw it when we were coming this way. It'll pull down, and there's stairs attached. We've got the same thing at home."

"Right, so we've got to get back out into the hall and to that attic thing, tug it down, climb the stairs, get up into the attic, and then get out through one of those windows up there and onto the roof?" Malik shrugged as casually as he could. "Piece of cake." Everybody laughed, which made him feel a little better. As long as they kept their heads they'd be okay, he kept telling himself. And keeping a sense of humor was part of that.

"Yeah, just one little problem," Christopher said as he looked pointedly at the bedroom door, the water flowing in from under its bottom edge. The floor was already getting squishy under their feet, and in a few more minutes they'd be immersed up to their ankles.

Which would be fine if the water weren't still flowing, but Malik could already feel it tugging at him. If they had to slog through that, back against the current into the hall, would they really be able to manage it?

He studied the room. "We could shove towels against the door," he suggested after a second, "to try to slow the water down. But the second we open the door—bam!"

"We don't want to bottle up the water," Jules agreed. "That's just going to make things worse once we have to step into it again. We need to . . . deflate it somehow. You know what I mean."

And Malik realized he did. She was exactly right— if the floodwaters pouring into this house were like air being pumped into a tire, they had to let that air back out before it crushed them. But how? If this were a tire, that'd be easy—they'd just poke a hole in it and let the air out that way. But this was a house, and putting holes in it was going to be a whole lot harder.

Except, he thought, that it had holes already. Built-in ones.

"Get the windows!" he shouted, rushing over to the closest one and yanking on it. It was stuck fast, but Christopher joined him, and together they were able to force it up an inch, then several more. "Open them wide! We'll let the water out that way!" The girls ran to the windows on the other wall, and a minute later

153

all the windows were up, letting rain spatter in from outside.

"Now what?" Ilyana asked.

"Get up on the dresser," Jules ordered. There were two dressers in the room—a tall, narrow one and a wide, shorter one—and it was the second one she indicated. They all stomped over to it, their footsteps making loud squelching sounds, and climbed up, shoving things out of their way. It was a tight squeeze, but the five of them were all able to fit on the dresser together.

Malik was right in front. "Everybody ready?" he called over his shoulder. Then he leaned down and twisted the doorknob before shoving the door open and toward the far wall.

As soon as it was unlatched, the water pressing against it took control, ripping the door out of his hands and sending it slamming into the wall. Water came sweeping into the room, quickly rising above what would have been ankle level, then knee level, then waist height. It was only a few inches below the dresser's top when the far edge hit the open window— and went pouring out of it.

Yes!

As Malik and his friends watched, more water entered the room, raced across it in a solid wave, and then went sailing out through the window without pause. The overall level never rose any higher—and, after a solid few minutes, it even began to drop.

It was working!

The water's surface was now lower than the windowsill, but there was still enough motion to cause a wave effect, which swept some of the water up high enough to let it soar over the window's edge anyway.

After a few more minutes, the water was back down to knee height, and the waves had all but stopped. The water was still now, though it was dangerously high.

Still, they'd have to chance it.

"We're going to climb back down off the dresser together," Malik told the others. "Don't try to go anywhere yet; just worry about getting down and putting both feet solidly on the ground." He turned and lowered himself carefully into the water, shuddering a little as his foot sank beneath the surface. But thanks to the rain boots Mr. Enright had given him, Malik's foot stayed mostly dry, and when he was standing again the water missed the top of the boots by an inch or two.

"Everybody good?" he asked, glancing at his classmates. They each gave him a thumbs-up. "Right. Grab onto the person in front of you. We're gonna have to go slow and carefully, just in case there's still a current, but that's alright. It's not a race." He turned and reached out to latch onto the door frame. Behind him, he felt Christopher grab his hood, which was hanging loose on his shoulders. "Good? Let's go."

And, putting one foot carefully in front of the other, moving slowly so Christopher could hold onto him, Malik waded out of the room.

It was slow going. The carpet was now so thoroughly soaked that it was coming up off the floor in some areas, which made it a bit treacherous, and Malik had to be sure his feet were on parts that were still solid. The water was still, fortunately, but there was so much of it that fighting his way through was like slogging through a wall of taffy, the liquid tugging at him with each step. A part of Malik realized he should have let Jules or Tracey go in front—both of them were bigger and more solid than he was—but he was already here, and he'd been the one with the plan, so they just had to keep going with it now.

And they did. Bit by bit, step by step, inch by inch, they made their way down the hall.

There was the ceiling hatch, just as Jules had said. A long cord hung down from it, but Malik was a little too short to grab it without jumping, and he was afraid to try that—what if he came down wrong and went under? Especially with the stairs right next to him, and everything hard to see under the water, he didn't want to risk it.

Fortunately, he didn't have to. "Keep moving," Jules called from the back. "I've got this." Malik kept going, working his way past the hatch far enough that first Christopher, then Ilyana, then Tracey, and finally Jules could also find space out in the hall. When Jules was right under the hatch, she called out "Stop!" and they all did.

Then she reached up and, with the ease of someone who'd done this many times before, grabbed the cord and hauled the hatch down in a single smooth tug.

It creaked and screeched so loudly that at first Malik thought something was wrong, but Jules didn't react at all, so perhaps they all did that? The hatch was hinged at the end closest to the master bedroom, and it was the other end—the one closer to them—that lowered, revealing a hinged staircase bolted onto it. Once the hatch was open completely, Jules caught hold of a second cord, which was connected to the stairs themselves, and pulled them down as well. They made a loud click as the two halves locked into place.

Jules didn't wait any longer. As soon as she heard that sound, she grabbed the built-in railing and started to haul herself up onto the stairs. It only took two steps before she was out of the water.

The rest of them followed her carefully, trying not to crowd after her but all eager to get someplace dry again.

Malik was the last up. The stairs wobbled a bit, which made him grip the railing tighter, but he'd seen everyone else ascend without a problem, so he just gulped and kept going. A few seconds later, he was standing in the attic with his classmates, dripping all over the rough plank floor.

"Epic!" Christopher declared, clapping him on the back. The other boy laughed. "Dude, that plan was boss!"

Malik couldn't help smiling. "Yeah, it worked great," he agreed. He glanced over at Jules. "Good thing you spotted those stairs—and knew how to operate 'em." She smiled back at him.

They all examined their new surroundings. The attic was completely dry, which was a nice change, although it smelled both musty from disuse and humid from all the recent rainfall. Boxes littered the floor, most of them labeled things like "winter sweaters" and "old toys" and "books—history." A few toys were scattered around as well. Most of the things had been grouped off to the sides, leaving plenty of room around the stairs in the center.

And, on other side, there were two windows jutting out, breaking up the slope of the roof. They rose from the floor of the attic, low enough that the kids would have to stoop or maybe even crawl to get to them, but

Malik thought they looked big enough for all of them to fit through.

Of course, judging from the drumbeat over their heads, and the droplets exploding against the windows, it was still pouring out. So they were going to have to climb out there in the middle of the storm, find something to hold onto, and then figure out what to do from there.

If it wasn't one thing, it was another!

CHAPTER 17

GETTING THE SIGNAL

"Hold up," Jules said, raising her hands like she was blocking the others from the goal—or, in this case, from climbing out the window. Not that any of them looked too eager to start on that anyway, but it was better to not take chances. "Before we go out there, we need a game plan."

"Seriously?" Tracey looked at her like she was nuts. "A game plan? This ain't no game!"

"I know, I know," Jules assured her friend, "but it still holds. We've got to know what we're doing, what we want to do, and how we aim to get there before we even crack that window. Otherwise"—she flung her hands out to the side like they'd exploded—"we lose."

Malik, surprisingly, was the one who nodded. "You're right," he said, which surprised her further. "It's still ugly out, so we'd better know what we're doing before we start having to fight off the wind and rain and flooding and everything else." He turned to Jules. "What've you got in mind?"

Honestly, Jules hadn't thought much further into her plan than the need to have a plan, but now she did. "Well, Mr. Enright and Dr. Lang and the others've got to be looking for us, right?" she asked.

"Sure," Christopher answered. "When the reservoir gave way, they'd have known we were still down here. They'd come running. Or swimming, maybe." He brushed his hair back out of his eyes and half smiled. At least he could still joke, Jules thought.

"They know we're down here, yeah," Tracey pointed out. "But not which house we went into. Or even if we're still in one. That's got to be our first priority, letting them know exactly where we are."

"Definitely," Jules said. "Half of the adults are probably out working on the reservoir, or the pumps, or headed this way, but they'd have left somebody back at that big tent, right? To coordinate everybody? So we should focus on that. Get whoever's in the tent to see where we are, and they'll let everyone else know."

"Calling's out," Ilyana informed them. She'd pulled out her cell phone and was holding it up, waving it around as if that would help somehow. "No signal. Rain might've washed away the cell towers or taken down the power to them . . . or something."

"Can't really light a fire either," Malik added, peering out the window at the rain. "And I guess we shouldn't be lighting up other folks' homes, anyways."

"Not with fire, no," Jules replied, something about what he'd just said sticking in her head. "But maybe we can light them up some other way. Like with a spotlight. That'd pretty much scream 'hey, we're here, come rescue us,' wouldn't it?"

"You got a spotlight hidden under the slicker somewhere?" Tracey asked her. "Because I definitely don't see one laying around here."

Jules scanned the attic as well, and her eyes lit as she spotted a tall, narrow piece of furniture standing against several boxes. "No, but this could work." She crossed the room and reached out to grab the standing mirror.

"Hey, yeah!" Ilyana agreed. "We can catch the sun's reflection and bounce it toward the tent! That'll work!" Her face fell. "Except for all those big rain clouds hanging over us."

"Sunlight would've been good," Jules responded, lifting the mirror and carrying it back over to the others. It wasn't heavy at all, even with its frame and the feet at the bottom of that. "But we can manage without it. We've all got a flashlight app, right?" Ilyana, Tracey, and Christopher all agreed. Malik looked crushed, and Jules remembered what had happened to his phone. She felt a little bad about that but couldn't worry about it too much at the moment, so she pushed on ahead. "If we all aim our phones at the mirror together, that should be bright enough."

She hoped.

Everyone else seemed to like the idea. "Let's do it," Malik declared. "Since that stupid old fissure ate my phone, I'll hold the mirror and aim it at the tent while the rest of you flash it."

There wasn't much else to say to that, so Jules lifted the mirror and tucked it under one arm while Tracey forced the nearest window open, kicked out the screen, and then climbed out. The rest of them followed her, with Malik going last in case Jules, right in front of him, needed any help maneuvering the mirror out through that narrow opening.

Jules appreciated the offer, but she wound up not needing it. The mirror fit through easily, and she was able to hand it off to Christopher—who was right ahead of her—squeeze her way out through the window, hoist herself up and find her balance on the roof, and then accept the mirror back from him.

Fortunately, the roof wasn't steeply angled—it had a gentler slope. And it was shingled, the shingles thick and sturdy and solidly attached, so much so that she was able to hook her heels into two shingles, anchoring herself in place.

Which was a good thing, because out here the wind was even fiercer than she'd noticed from inside,

and the shingles were slick with a constant stream of water, making her feet slip and slide across them. The only way up was to wedge her feet against the shingles and then lift one foot at a time and search for the next place to plant herself. Tracey was already at the peak, feet straddling it firmly, and was hauling Ilyana up beside her when Malik emerged and half climbed, half jumped from the window to the roof proper.

"Oof!" he grunted as he landed hard and had to grab onto an edge of the window's roof to keep from toppling. "Hey, it's like PE and science class, all rolled into one!"

Jules laughed and shook her head. She didn't know how Malik could still joke at a time like this, but she was glad he was. It helped take her mind off exactly what they were doing, and why.

Christopher was up at the peak now and extended a hand to Jules to help her along. She passed him the mirror first, then took his hand and let him guide her along. With her own free hand she reached back to Malik, and the three of them formed a chain that slowly crept its way to the top of the roof, where their other two classmates were waiting.

"Right, which way is the tent?" Malik asked once they were all together again. "I'm all turned around."

So was Jules, but peering down she could just make out the front sidewalk leading up to this house. And if that was there, they must have come from over that way, which meant where they'd climbed the hill was about there and the tent should be right about . . . "There!" she shouted, pointing. She'd caught just the barest flash of white, but she knew she was right. "It's right there!"

Malik frowned, following her finger, then smiled. "Got it!" He took the mirror from Christopher and angled it toward the tent, which was only barely visible through the driving rain. "Okay, everybody ready?"

The rest of them got out their phones and activated their flashlight apps, then aimed them at the mirror.

"When I say 'go,' hit the lights, then click them off again," Malik instructed. "We'll do that three times. Then turn them on when I say to, but leave them on until I say 'off.' That'll be another three times, then three more where you just hit the lights and then immediately kill them again. Got it?"

"Three short, three long, three short," Ilyana confirmed. "That's an S.O.S.!"

S.O.S. is an international distress signal. It was first used in Germany in the early twentieth century, after Morse code was developed, and was quickly adopted worldwide. Contrary to popular myth, the letters were chosen for how easy they are to "write" in Morse code and do not stand for "save our souls" or "save our ship."

"Exactly!" Malik replied. "My dad taught me that the first time we went camping." He looked around at everyone. "Ready?" They all said they were, and Malik took a deep breath and then shouted, "Go!"

Four flashlight apps came to life all at once and turned toward the mirror, which caught and intensified the blazes of light into a single big burst.

Following Malik's directions, they switched their lights on and off, on and off, in the prescribed pattern. Jules didn't dare turn to look behind her, but if anyone was watching from the tent, she was sure they'd see the display, even with all the rain.

They had to!

"Should we do it again?" Ilyana asked once they'd finished and turned their phones back off. "In case they missed it the first time?"

Jules considered that. "Not yet," she decided finally. "We don't want to waste the batteries and have nothing left. Let's give them a few minutes. It's not like they can just drive on over to pick us up."

Even so, she stared out into the gloom, straining to pierce the rain and fog that blocked out most of the world more than a few feet away. Had anyone seen their signal? What if nobody did? What if nobody came for them? Forcing thoughts like that from her head, Jules made herself focus on the positive, the biggest of which was this: She was not here alone.

They all huddled together against the rain, concentrating on the white tent and watching for any hint of movement.

Nothing.

Jules's shoulders slumped. They were going to be stuck here forever!

Just then, Malik put a hand on her shoulder. "It's going to be okay," he assured her. "It really will."

Jules wiped at her eyes, which seemed to have gotten some rainwater in them. "How do you know?" she demanded. "You can't be sure."

He just shrugged. "Why not?" he asked her, smiling at some joke he was about to share. "It sure beats the alternative, right?"

That made Jules laugh again. The others joined in, laughing way more than that silly little joke had warranted. Their humor was tinged with madness, maybe, at how crazy this whole day had been already. But it still felt good to let it all out.

They were still gasping for breath and trying to stop when Jules thought she heard something over their laughter. Something deeper and rougher and louder than their voices.

Something that she spotted a minute or so later as a long, dark shape raced toward them, not through the water but on top of it.

"Look!" she yelled out. Everybody turned to stare and then started hollering and screaming once they saw it.

It was a boat.

And it was heading right for them.

They were saved!

CHAPTER 18

RESCUE MISSION

The boat wasn't one of those long, sleek, dart-like vessels you often saw in movies and on TV shows, Malik noticed as it approached. In fact, it was almost exactly the opposite—wide and flat, with what looked like an enormous fan mounted on the back. And instead of plush leather seats and an ultra-high-tech console, it had a single chair mounted up high right in front of the fan, and then the sides basically flared out at their tops to form low benches just above the water. It was old and battered, and the fan made a loud whir that was audible even over the rain.

Even so, it was the most beautiful thing Malik had ever seen.

And equally welcome was the tall man piloting it in his bright yellow rain slicker—and the smaller but similarly dressed figure hopping up and down at the front of the boat.

"There you all are!" Mr. Enright called out as he expertly banked the boat, pulling it up so its side bumped gently against the side of the house. He killed the engine, the fan slowing to a stop, and then tossed something like a squishy softball at the side of the house. The strange object stuck there, and Malik realized that it was attached to a sturdy rope tied to large eyelets along the boat's side. It was like an instant anchor, one that could attach to anything. Sweet.

"Bud and I have been searching for you everywhere," their teacher continued, leaning back in his seat. Oddly, he looked completely at home on the old, beaten-up boat, even though Malik could see Mr. Enright's dress pants sticking out of his rain boots. "We knew you were somewhere around here, but we weren't sure where exactly—not until they spotted your signal and relayed it to me."

Malik and his classmates exchanged high-fives. It had worked!

"Well, hop aboard," Mr. Enright instructed. "Let's get you out of here, eh?"

They had no argument there! The water level was high enough that the boat was only a few inches below the roof's bottom edge, and Mr. Enright reached up and helped them down into the boat, one at a time. It rocked a little with each new person, and Malik gulped when it was his turn. But the boat was surprisingly steady, and its wide, flat deck had plenty of space to fit them all.

The minute he was across, Bud was all over Malik.

The chimp wrapped both arms around his neck and both legs around his waist, hauling himself up onto Malik like he was a small tree. Then the chimp gave him a big, wet kiss—right on the lips!

"Yeah, yeah, I missed you too," Malik spluttered, wiping his lips on his sleeve. The others just laughed.

"He's definitely bonded with you," Mr. Enright commented, chuckling along with everyone else. "But we're both happy to see all of you. I'm terribly sorry about all of that—we thought it would be perfectly safe."

"What happened?" Jules asked.

"The reservoir burst," their teacher replied, which was exactly what they'd guessed. "The sandbags were not enough to hold all that water back, and it overflowed. Then of course the water came crashing right back onto the floodplain—exactly where you were."

"Yeah, we noticed," Malik said. But he couldn't really be too mad at anyone. It had been an honest mistake.

Besides, they were all okay.

Well, most of them.

"Where is Randall?" Mr. Enright asked as if reading his mind.

The kids all exchanged glances.

"He thought we should try to swim to safety once

173

the water hit," Tracey answered finally. "He wanted all of us to go with him, but there was no way." She shrugged. "So he dove in on his own. That was the last we saw of him."

Mr. Enright frowned. "He'd have tried for the tent, surely," he mused aloud. "But they've not seen hide nor hair of him." He peered out at the flooded neighborhood. "He could be anywhere by now."

"Maybe not," Jules said. She was staring off in the distance toward the white spot Malik knew was the command tent. "We were in the kitchen, right?" she recalled. "And Randall dove into the water facing straight ahead from that door, which means he was pointed that way." She gestured behind them, past the rear of the boat and toward the rest of the neighborhood. "Which way is the water flowing?"

"That way," Ilyana answered, pointing to their left, across the house—the same way this boat had been heading. That made sense; Mr. Enright must have been riding the current rather than fighting it, so he'd been working his way downstream toward them.

"Okay." Jules frowned. "So if he started out going straight ahead, and the water was pulling him to the left, he should be somewhere in that direction." The area she was indicating ranged from directly behind the boat to exactly left of the house, which Malik knew was one-fourth of the floodplain.

"That's a lot of area to cover," he commented. "You really think we'll find him?"

But Jules wasn't done. "We can narrow it down," she replied. "There's no way Randall could fight the current completely, right? It was just too strong. Which means he can't be straight ahead. And the farther he got, the more it would've pulled him to the left. But the nearest houses are right across the street— that's what, twenty feet? That's close enough that he'd still be making some headway, especially if he's a strong swimmer."

"Which he is," Christopher added. "He wanted to be a SEAL, remember?"

"So you're saying he's got to be more like—there?" Malik asked. He waved his hand toward the middle portion of the quadrant—if it had been on a clock face, with straight ahead as twelve and directly left at nine, they were looking at between ten and eleven. And there were two houses in plain sight that way, back to back on the near end of the next block. "So he should be in one of those two," Malik finished.

Jules nodded. "Yeah. At least, I think so." She glanced down at her booted feet, unusually unsure of herself, and Malik felt bad for her.

"Makes sense to me," he told her. She rewarded his support with a shy smile he liked a whole lot more than her usual confident bluster.

"To me as well," Mr. Enright agreed from his perch. "Well reasoned, Jules! That's using geometry and physics to solve our little problem." He flipped a switch, and the boat's fan spun back to life. "Someone collect our anchor line," he shouted over the noise, "and let's go see if we can't retrieve our teacher's aide, eh?"

The kids all cheered. Christopher was closest to the house, so he reached out and, with a few grunts and tugs, managed to wrestle the sticky rope end off the wall. The rest of them found seats along the boat's lip, latching onto handgrips installed at intervals around the edge for clearly just such a purpose.

"Everyone ready?" Mr. Enright called down. When he saw they were, he pushed forward on the long lever at his side, and the boat shot forward across the water. Then he tugged the lever and the whole vessel swiveled around, cutting a sharp curve around the house and then aiming across the street toward the two houses Jules had targeted.

The ones they really hoped held their missing member.

The first house looked like a bust even before they'd reached it—it was completely dark, which made sense since the power was out all across the neighborhood, but it also had all of its windows and doors closed tight. If Randall had taken refuge there, why would he have shut the window behind him?

They cruised slowly around the house anyway, shining light through the windows with sturdy flashlights Mr. Enright handed them. But it looked dark and deserted.

"Right, on to house number two!" their teacher yelled, steering the boat toward the neighboring house.

At first glance, that one didn't look any more promising. But then Ilyana perked up. "Look!" she shouted. "There!" They all followed her finger—to an open window on the second floor.

"I'll get us closer," Mr. Enright declared. And, with impressive skill, he maneuvered the boat up against that window, just barely tapping the wall. "Just like that time in Chile," Malik heard him mutter, "only without the sharks, of course."

Malik was too busy peering in through the window to figure out what his teacher was going on about. "Randall?" he called out instead. "Randall, you in there?"

The others all joined him in shouting Randall's name.

Then Malik heard it. A faint reply. Coming from somewhere inside the house!

"He's in there!" Malik shouted over his shoulder. He was all set to dive in through the window and go after Randall when a hand on his shoulder stopped him. It was Jules.

"We don't know what's in there," she pointed out. "He could be stuck, and if you go after him you might get stuck, too. Not a good plan."

"So what do we do?" Malik asked her. "We can't just leave him in there!"

"I believe someone else has the answer to that," Mr. Enright said. He glanced to Malik's side and Malik turned, looking down at Bud, who stood beside him. Grinning. And holding, in one hand, the sticky end of the anchor line.

"Bud!" Ilyana said, clapping her hands. "That's epic! You can get in and out if we can't!"

"And he's got the rope, so he could use that to lead Randall back out," Christopher added. "Smart."

With a quick grunt and a chirp, Bud leaped in through the window. He was able to clear its sides easily. Malik thought for a second that the chimp was going to splash down into the water, which he could see was at least waist high, and he had a moment of panic. Could Bud even swim? But the former astronaut had no intention of getting dunked. Instead, Bud reached out with one long arm and grabbed ahold of the room's ceiling fan, swinging himself up and across until he landed on what looked like a dresser against the far wall.

"That was sick," Malik whispered. The chimp bobbed his head and beamed as if he'd heard the compliment. Then he saluted, turned, and disappeared through the door, presumably down the hall.

Malik and the others waited tensely. Was Bud okay? Would he be able to find Randall? Was Randall okay? Would he be able to reach them?

After a few minutes, Malik caught a flash of red from inside. "I see him!" he called out. The others all crowded around.

Sure enough, a red-suited figure was making its way toward them, slogging through the water. Which only came up to its waist. That couldn't possibly be Bud, which meant it was . . . Randall!

But as he drew closer, Malik saw that the teacher's aide wasn't alone. He was holding onto the anchor line, reeling himself back toward the window and the boat beyond, but the rope rose back up over his shoulder, looping around to a smaller figure perched on his shoulders and banging on his head like it was a drum.

Bud!

"Rescue team successful," Randall declared as he reached the window. "Good work, soldiers. Commendations all around." Bud scampered off his shoulders and through the window back onto the boat, and then the teacher's aide pulled himself through the opening and followed. He saluted Mr. Enright once he was on the boat properly, and their teacher returned the gesture without the slightest hint of a smirk.

"Permission to come aboard, sir!" Randall requested with all of his usual volume. It looked like

he wasn't any worse off from his experience!

"Permission granted, son," Mr. Enright replied, smirking now, but not meanly. "Got caught up in the current, did you?"

"Sir, yes sir," Randall shouted back. "Carried me out of true, sir! Made it as far as that house, thought I'd wait until the water lowered a bit before trying again, sir! But then you arrived to retrieve me, thank you." That last bit sounded less like a military parade and more like an ordinary guy saying thanks for being rescued, and for just a second Malik thought Randall might not be so bad. Then the teacher's aide snapped to attention again. "What are our orders now, sir?"

Mr. Enright laughed. "I think we'd best be getting back, don't you?" he asked all of them. "We'll head to the command tent, let Dr. Lang know we're alright, return his boat, and then head back to school."

"Roger that—debriefing it is!" Randall declared, and Malik groaned.

Why had they been so eager to rescue this guy?

CHAPTER 19

FOND FAREWELLS

"I am so sorry!" Dr. Lang said as soon as Mr. Enright had ushered them all back into the command tent. "We had no idea that would happen—if we'd known, we never would have let you kids go down there like that!"

"Eh, accidents happen," Malik replied, like it was no big deal they'd all almost drowned! But Jules didn't make a big deal out of it, either. After all, they'd survived just fine. And they'd done it on their own, which was actually kind of neat.

"So, what, it was just too much water for the sandbags to hold back?" Christopher asked.

Dr. Lang and the other adults all looked embarrassed. "That's exactly what it was," the project leader agreed. "I'm afraid we underestimated the amount of water we were dealing with and overestimated our makeshift reservoir's strength and capacity. The more water we pumped in, the more pressure was put on those sandbags, and eventually they just gave way. Once the first one toppled, well, you've heard the expression 'the dam burst'?" The kids all nodded. "That's exactly what happened here. All that pressure went shooting out through the opening, faster than we could try to contain it again. And it all poured right back down onto the floodplain—right on your heads."

"And here we thought that was the rain!" Malik joked, shaking his head. "Hey, maybe a bunch of smaller reservoirs would work better next time?"

"That's exactly what we realized after it failed," the civil engineer, Tanya, agreed. "So we reconfigured everything into five smaller reservoirs, and now we're busy pumping all that water back up again. As soon as one reservoir starts getting full, we switch to the next one, so even if one does give way again it won't have nearly the same effect as before."

"Nice," Tracey remarked. "We'd offer to help some more, but—" she gestured down at herself, and then at the rest of them.

For the first time since they'd started all this, Jules looked closely at their class. They were a mess! All of them were still wearing their bright slickers and rain boots, but they were now caked in dirt and mud. Most of them were soaking wet under the rain gear from diving under water or falling, or just having to wade through it all. Their hair was sticking out all over the place from being trapped in those hoods and subjected to all that water and humidity and wind, and their faces and hands were smudged and dirty as well. They looked like—well, they looked like they'd just survived a flash flood!

"Yes, I believe it is time to return to school, and then to your respective homes," Mr. Enright agreed. "I do feel we've learned a great deal today, and I thank you, Henry, for allowing my students to get some real hands-on experience here."

"My pleasure," Dr. Lang replied. He came around and shook each of their hands in turn. "We really appreciate you guys coming out here. It's not often that we get to explain what we do, and it's especially nice to see kids getting interested in science and math."

"Plus a lot of your suggestions were really great!" Rachel the ecologist added cheerfully. "I think having you guys join us today really made a difference!" She and the other adults all came over to say good-bye to everyone. It was pretty sweet, and Jules was still waving at people as Mr. Enright led them back out of the tent. Bud had taken Malik's hand again, as usual, and Randall was once more bringing up the rear and barking at Ilyana, who was right in front of him, to keep up.

The rain was starting to let up, finally, and spots of blue were peeking through the clouds as the kids made their way back to the bus. "Do you think they'll be able to get all the water out now?" Jules asked as they walked.

"Oh, I'd imagine so," Mr. Enright answered, stepping carefully around a spot where they couldn't see the pavement through the water. "Those pumps were already going great guns, and if this rain really does stop they won't have to worry about any additional moisture, so they can concentrate on what's already on the ground. Plus, they did manage to repair the first reservoir in time to retain some of what they'd captured, which means they had a bit of a head start this time around."

"They can't keep pumps around the edge of the floodplain all the time, though, right?" Ilyana asked. "I mean, what's going to happen if it pours like this again? I know they're going to make the houses more flood-proof, but that won't stop water from filling up the streets."

"Yeah. That one guy, Mike, said they could maybe use fissures to drain off the water when it flooded," Malik remembered, "but he said those only formed on higher ground, so that could keep water from pouring down onto the floodplain from the hills, but it won't help if the floodplain itself fills up."

"Didn't somebody say something about a wall?" Christopher offered. "A low wall around the floodplain to keep the water from washing in?"

"Right, they did," Jules confirmed, remembering the conversation. "But they said it'd take a while to build something like that, and that the water would still wash over it if there was enough flooding." She frowned. "There's got to be a way to make sure those houses are safe!"

But their teacher shook his head. "Unfortunately, there's no perfect solution," he told them. "The real problem is that a floodplain is the natural place for water to pool. So everything we do to prevent that is us trying to fight Mother Nature, and that's an uphill battle—that means it's harder because we're going against the way things naturally work. If we were building a whole new neighborhood on a floodplain, then yes, there are some things we could do. Like add a drainage system."

"That's when the water all drains out from underneath, right?" Tracey asked. "Like in a shower or a bathtub?"

Mr. Enright looked pleased. "Precisely! We cannot drill down into the ground itself because we're already at the lowest point, so there aren't tunnels and canals below for the water to drain off into. But if we were starting from scratch, we could lay down a full system of drains and pipes and then lay the road and ground on top of that." He shrugged. "That's not something we could do here, though—not without tearing down all these homes and then ripping up all these roads."

"Could they build a water tower to collect the water as it falls?" Ilyana wanted to know. "Would that help?"

"It could," their teacher answered, "especially if they somehow funneled any water from the surrounding hills down into that tower. That way there wouldn't be more water descending up the neighborhood. A tower wouldn't be able to stop water from falling across the rest of the floodplain, however. Not unless you extended its tubes to cover the entire neighborhood!"

Jules was thinking about how the water had tried to force the door to the master bedroom open when they'd been hiding in there, and how as soon as they'd opened the door the water had come pouring in—and then had rushed right out the open window. That had to do with the pressure, she remembered. "Is there some way we could force water on the ground into a tube leading up to a water tower?" she asked. "I don't mean pumping it up there, but making it go on its own? By putting pressure behind it?"

"You mean like an artesian well?" Mr. Enright asked her. "Hmm." He stroked his chin. "That's a very interesting idea, Jules. If the water tower was at the lowest point on the floodplain, and had intake tubes on the ground all around it, when the water started to fill up there it'd be putting intense pressure on the water closest to those tubes. The water would be forced into the tubes and then up and out of sight. Yes, very clever." He favored her with a warm, proud look. "I will suggest that to Dr. Lang—and be sure to credit you for the idea—just as soon as we get back."

Jules beamed. It had been cool enough helping stop that leak at school the other day, and even sweeter helping with that house earlier, but the thought that something she'd said could wind up helping dozens of people and their homes, maybe all over the country? That was seriously epic.

She was still floating from excitement and pride when they finally reached the school bus. It was sitting exactly where they'd left it, and as soon as they got within sight, Bud squealed with delight and went racing toward the bus. Not to be outdone, Malik started after the chimp as quickly as he could manage. Soon they were all racing for the school bus, laughing and hollering as they went. It was like a party, a race, and a field trip, all rolled into one!

Bud still reached the parked vehicle first. He did something to the door, and it slid open just enough for him to squeeze past. He hopped right up onto the driver's seat, nodded with his big, toothy grin, and pulled the door lever. The doors opened the rest of the way and they all piled in, dropping into seats with exhausted sighs. Jules was as loud as the rest of them—she felt like she'd just finished a championship tournament, playing three games back to back! In the rain! While fending off a pack of wild, hungry bears!

It had definitely been an amazing day, but she was more than ready to let it end!

CHAPTER 20

OVERSIGHT

By the time they got back to school, the rain had completely stopped and many of the clouds had already drifted apart. Those that remained were a lighter shade and far less angry-looking than the furious thunderclouds they'd all been living under for the past few days.

"It's a good thing we went when we did," Mr. Enright commented from his seat right behind Bud, as the bus swerved around a corner and sent water flying onto the sidewalk beside it. "Another few hours, even, and we'd not have had any flooding at all!" Malik thought it was a little odd that their teacher was so happy they'd had a disaster to go visit, but he understood what the man meant. They could have stayed at school and studied flash floods, of course, but that wouldn't have been anywhere near as interesting as seeing one in person—and up close!

At the very least, Malik was sure this was a field trip none of them would ever forget—and that he'd always remember what he'd learned today too!

They got back to school without incident, the bus depositing them at the front doors this time. But when the bus had come to a complete stop and Bud had tugged on the lever, the bus door opened to reveal someone already standing there waiting.

And it wasn't one of their parents.

"Mister Enright!" Doctor Pillai bellowed, her voice surprisingly loud for someone shorter than at least half of her students. "Where the heck have you been?" Judging from her tone, and the way her face was bright red, Malik was pretty sure she'd wanted to say something a whole lot more severe than "heck."

"We went to investigate the floodplain," their teacher answered, hopping down from the bus and towering over his boss. "It was highly informative."

"It was highly dangerous!" The principal snapped. "I got a call from Dr. Lang an hour or two ago—he said your entire class went missing!"

"Ah, yes. Well there was a momentary lapse in communication—" Mr. Enright began, but she cut him off before he could get any further.

"A momentary lapse is someone not answering their cell phone," she practically snarled up at him, "or running off to the bathroom without telling anyone. An entire class disappearing into a flood zone without adult supervision is something entirely different!"

Surprisingly, Randall spoke up. "Sorry to correct

you, sir," he stated, "but, in fact, the students were accompanied by an adult at all times. I was supervising them out in the field."

That only earned him a glare from Dr. Pillai, however. "You're eighteen," she pointed out. "So, yes, technically you're an adult, in that you're old enough to vote and drive and so on. But you're still a college kid, barely older than they are, so no, I don't see that as being any better. If anything, it makes matters worse, because if something'd happened to all of you, I'd have to explain it to your college dean as well."

"Well, they're all here now, and none the worse for wear," their teacher pointed out, trying to smile reassuringly but not managing it very well. "See for yourself." He gestured at the bus, where Malik and the others had all crowded around the door to watch the two adults argue.

But the principal wasn't satisfied. "That is not the point!" she insisted loudly, wagging a finger at him. "You were responsible for them, and you not only let them go somewhere dangerous, but you also put them right smack in the middle of it! And then left them there! That is unacceptable!"

"It wasn't dangerous when they went out into it," Mr. Enright tried again, though he sounded less confident and a bit more wheedling. "We all thought they would be perfectly safe. No one could have predicted that the reservoir would break."

"Break?" He actually winced at her shout. "It broke? You took your students—*my* students—to a floodplain and the reservoir broke?" She looked ready to strangle him. "It's amazing they survived! And if their parents decide to sue, it'll be a miracle if *we* survive!"

"Sue?" That was Ilyana, who poked her head out to speak to the principal. "Why would anyone sue? We had a great time! I learned lots about flooding, and ecology, and civil engineering, and all kinds of stuff! It was epic!"

The rest of them all chimed in, agreeing, and Mr. Enright straightened. It was clear that their enthusiasm and support had revived him.

"There, you see?" he told Dr. Pillai. "No one's going to get sued, everyone is fine, and they had an excellent—and highly educational—time. When was the last time you saw students this enthused about science, hm?"

The principal harrumphed but apparently didn't have an argument for that.

"I might also remind you," their teacher added, "that this program is independently funded, and thus has a certain degree of autonomy. The school board approved the plan, and as long as I don't deviate from that I am well within my purview. And spontaneous field trips to locales where scientists and other experts are using their skills and knowledge to deal with problems is the centerpiece of the curriculum."

"That still doesn't mean you can put them at risk!" Dr. Pillai sputtered out, though she'd clearly lost her momentum now.

"That was an oversight," Mr. Enright admitted, "and I assure you that it will not happen again. Adults were all over the area—all of them experts in their fields—including several city officials. It does not get much safer than that. We simply miscalculated— it happens. But the children handled themselves admirably, and they were retrieved as quickly as possible."

Their principal sighed and squeezed the bridge of her nose between her thumb and forefinger the way Malik had seen his mom do when he and his sister were getting on her nerves. "I don't know," she said, more quietly, this time. "I think this may just be too much to handle. Maybe if we shelve it for a year or two, and come back to it, then . . ."

Malik found himself holding his breath. A year or two? That would mean getting sent back to his boring old science class instead! And even if they did manage to start this class up again—and he knew that "maybe later" was often adult-code for "it'll never happen"—

he and the others would probably be too old to take it by then!

He couldn't believe it, but he was actually worried about whether they'd get to keep their science class!

Fortunately, Mr. Enright didn't seem too worried by the principal's suggestion. "If that's how you really feel," he started slowly, dragging each word out a bit, "I suppose I could speak to her about it. Let her know your . . . concerns and get her take on the situation. You know how she likes to get personally involved."

Dr. Pillai actually shuddered and took a step back. "No, no," she said quickly, "that's fine. Let's not bother her with all this." She shook her head. "Fine, you can keep the class. For now. But I'll be watching, and there'd better not be any more screwups!"

And with that, the principal turned and stormed back into the school.

Mr. Enright watched her go and then glanced at the kids, who were still huddled in the bus door, a bit confused about all this "her" business. "Right," he announced briskly. "Let's go down and gather your things and then see about getting you all home, shall we? It's been a busy day, and I'd imagine you're wanting a breather. And some dry clothes."

Malik laughed, relieved that the argument was over and the class was staying, and spilled out of the bus with the others. They followed their teacher down the now-empty halls to classroom 103, then through the fake wall to the elevator and down to 103b.

Their classroom.

He didn't know when he'd come to think of it that way, but it was definitely theirs.

When the elevator doors slid open, Bud pushed past the rest of them and darted off down the hall. Which was strange, Malik thought. He tried not to be upset that his chimpanzee buddy had taken off on him like that. Maybe he had to use the bathroom?

But when they entered the classroom, Bud was right there, waiting for them.

And he was not alone.

CHAPTER 21

A SURPRISE

"Ah, there you are, my dear!" the woman sitting at the front of the room called out as they entered. Jules had never seen her before, but there was something vaguely familiar about her long, narrow features; long nose; and black hair. She was wearing a white lab coat over cargo shorts and a brightly colored Hawaiian shirt, and Bud was perched on the counter beside her, smiling. Jules noticed that the woman had one arm around the chimpanzee like they were old friends.

But who was she? And what was she doing here? Was this "her"?

"Hello, auntie," Mr. Enright replied, striding over and giving the woman a quick one-armed hug and a peck on the cheek. That explained it, Jules thought. She looks like him! "I wasn't expecting you."

"No, I was in town testing my new amphibious bike and thought I'd pop in," she replied. "It all looks very good," she added, glancing around the room.

Amphibious means something that is suited to both land and water. Frogs are amphibious because they can live in both. An amphibious car would be able to drive on land but either sail across water or drive under water.

"They did a fine job."

"Well, you gave them very detailed plans to work from," their teacher pointed out. He turned back toward the kids. "Auntie, I'd like you to meet my class. This is Ilyana, Tracey, Malik, Jules, and Christopher. Oh, and Randall, my aide." Randall saluted, of course, but the woman surprised Jules by saluting back, her motions every bit as crisp as his. "Class," Mr. Enright continued, "this is my aunt, Nancy Enright."

Jules frowned. She'd heard that name somewhere before, hadn't she?

Malik evidently had. "Nancy Enright?" He asked. "As in, the head of Enright Engineering? And E-space? And Encom?"

"Yes, well," Nancy nodded, "I like to keep busy."

Jules gaped at the woman, as did the others. She'd seen the name Enright Engineering, though all she knew about it was that it built things like cars and maybe planes and stuff. But E-space was the leading Internet company in all the world. And Encom was the biggest communications company. And this woman owned all of them?

And she was Mr. Enright's aunt?

And what had that been about her providing the plans for this place?

"Aunt Nancy is the one behind this whole program," Mr. Enright explained as if reading Jules's mind. "Without her, there'd be no STEM class."

"Oh, p'shaw," his aunt muttered, pushing him away playfully. "It was your idea, Todd, not mine. I just thought it was a good one, so I funded it. And maybe pulled a few strings with the school board." She turned to the kids. "So, how are you liking it so far?"

"It's killer!" Malik replied. "Totally boss!"

"We're learning all kinds of stuff—and it's all real stuff for the real world," Ilyana added.

"Yeah, it's really amazing," Christopher added.

Tracey just nodded, like their classmates had already said everything that needed saying. Jules kind of agreed.

Mr. Enright was beaming at the compliments, and his aunt laughed and patted his arm proudly. "Good for you!" she told him. "Looks like it's going gangbusters!"

"Oh, it is," their teacher agreed happily. "And it's only the first week!"

"I'd love to stay and chat, but I'm afraid I've got a charity dinner tonight." Nancy hopped off her seat—now Jules noticed that it wasn't one of the regular stools but a strange contraption that looked like an inflatable chair on top of some kind of jointed mechanical column—and pushed a button just below the seat. Instantly it deflated, the column collapsing at the same time. By the time the woman bent over to pick it up, all that was left was a metal rod about the size of a large glow stick. "Portable chair," she explained. "My own invention. Never leave home without it." She straightened, tucking the rod into a pocket on her lab coat, and then rose on her tiptoes to give Mr. Enright a kiss on the cheek. "Lovely to see you, dear. So glad it's going well. Nice to meet all of you too. I'm sure I'll see you again soon."

They all called out good-bye as she crossed the room and headed out down the hall. Bud went with her but came back alone a minute or two later.

"Right, best call your folks and arrange to head home," Mr. Enright told everyone after his aunt had left. "If anyone needs a ride, we still have the bus and I'm sure Bud would be happy to drive some more." Jules giggled at that—so her thought earlier, about some of them being chauffeured home by a chimp, really might come true!

"Mr. Enright?" she asked after she'd called her parents and her mom had agreed to come and get her.

"Yes?" He'd been studying his clipboard but glanced up when he heard his name.

"This was great," Jules started, "but I was just wondering—what's next?"

"Yeah," Tracey agreed. "That flash flood's gonna be hard to top!"

To their surprise, their teacher just laughed. "Oh, I can think of a few things that would beat it hollow," he assured them. "But as to what's next?" He smiled widely. "I have absolutely no idea! There's a whole wide world out there," he continued, throwing his arms wide to take it all in, "and it's filled with science! And we're going to explore every last bit of it together!"

Jules chuckled at his antics. But as she and the others headed for the elevator, and home, she realized that she believed what Mr. Enright had promised.

And that she was looking forward to it.

STUDY GUIDE
Quiz

Okay, so you've finished reading the book. Congratulations! Now, how much of it do you remember? See how well you do on the following quiz—and no cheating and flipping back to figure out the answers (found on page 210)!

1. What is it doing on the first day of school?

   a. raining
   b. snowing
   c. sleeting
   d. sneezing

2. Who is the first STEM kid we meet?

   a. Jules
   b. Malik
   c. Ilyana
   d. Cell

3. What was the name of Malik's original science teacher?

   a. Mr. Carroway
   b. Mr. Carruthers
   c. Mrs. Cavanaugh
   d. Captain Caveman

4. Who does Malik overhear talking during lunch the first day?

   a. Jules and Tracey
   b. Bud and Mr. Enright
   c. Mr. Enright and Dr. Pillai
   d. His stomach and his lunch

5. Who is the second STEM kid we meet?

   a. Jules
   b. Malik
   c. Bud
   d. Brain

6. What is the STEM classroom number?

   a. 221b
   b. 120f
   c. 103b
   d. 9 3/4

7. How do you get to the actual STEM classroom?

   a. A hidden elevator
   b. A secret door
   c. A sliding panel
   d. A waterslide

8. What is Mr. Enright wearing when we first meet him?

   a. A lab coat
   b. A spacesuit
   c. A tuxedo
   d. A ghost costume

9. Who is waiting for the kids at the bottom of the elevator? What is he wearing?

   a. Bud in a flight suit
   b. Mr. Enright in a jumpsuit
   c. Randall in camo gear
   d. A camel in a flight vest

10. What is the first real-life problem the STEM class has to help solve?

    a. A broken door
    b. A leaky pipe
    c. A busted hose
    d. World peace

11. What bothers Chris the most about STEM class?

    a. No desks
    b. No books
    c. No guidelines
    d. No shoes

12. What is Randall's major?

    a. English
    b. Engineering
    c. Environmental science
    d. Enlightenment

13. What does Randall want to be when he graduates?

    a. A Navy SEAL
    b. A scientist
    c. An astronaut
    d. A rodeo clown

14. What is Jules's dad worried about with STEM class?

a. That it's too hard
b. That it's too easy
c. That it's distracting her from sports
d. That it's giving her pudding

15. What does Bud run into class to tell Mr. Enright about?

a. A flash flood
b. A flash mob
c. A camera flash
d. A super-fast superhero

16. Who is driving the STEM bus?

a. Mr. Enright
b. Randall
c. Bud
d. Their imaginary friend

17. Why do they leave the bus behind?

a. It gets a flat tire
b. The water's too high for it to go any farther
c. It runs out of gas
d. The color yellow is too distracting

18. Who is in charge of the Southern California Flood Crisis Management Team?

a. Mr. Enright
b. Bud
c. Dr. Lang
d. Captain Planet

19. What does Malik almost fall into?

a. A sinkhole
b. A manhole
c. A wormhole
d. A blowhole

20. Who saves him?

a. A stranger
b. Mr. Enright
c. Jules
d. The Lone Ranger

21. What does he lose in the process?

a. His phone
b. His lunch
c. His cool
d. His left shoe

22. What exciting news |does Bud bring when he re-enters the tent?

a. It's lunch time!
b. It's show time!
c. It stopped raining!
d. The ice cream truck is coming!

23. What do they send the kids down to help do?

a. Check houses for water damage
b. Look for anyone still trapped in the houses
c. Mark the walls where the water hit
d. Make sure no one has their dishwasher going

24. What goes wrong that sends more water cascading toward them?

a. It starts raining again
b. The reservoir breaks
c. A dam breaks
d. Someone turns on the shower

25. Whose idea is it to climb out onto the roof?

a. Tracey
b. Mr. Enright
c. Christopher
d. Prince Charming

26. What is Jules's idea on how to signal the scientists that they need help?

a. To call them
b. To send up smoke signals
c. To flash lights at them
d. To beam thoughts into their heads

27. What is the signal they send?

a. SOS
b. FTP
c. ROFL
d. UPS

28. Who pilots the boat that comes to find them?

    a. Dr. Lang
    b. Mr. Enright
    c. Bud
    d. James Bond

29. Who goes in to rescue Randall?

    a. All the kids
    b. Jules and Malik
    c. Bud
    d. Scooby Doo

30. Who do the kids meet when they get back to their classroom?

    a. The President
    b. Nancy Enright
    c. The head of NASA
    d. An alien

Quiz Answer Key

1. a	11. c	21. a
2. b	12. b	22. c
3. c	13. a	23. a
4. c	14. c	24. b
5. a	15. a	25. a
6. c	16. c	26. c
7. a	17. b	27. a
8. c	18. c	28. b
9. a	19. a	29. c
10. b	20. c	30. b

Discussion Questions

Here are a few questions you can discuss with your class about what happened in the book and why. These are less about remembering specific details or finding answers and more about sharing your own thoughts, ideas, and feelings about the characters and the story—and the science!

1. Why was Malik so excited at the start? Where was he going?

2. What is going on that makes Malik's trip unpleasant?

3. Where is Malik's family from? How do you know?

4. Judging from the first chapter, what kind of kid is Malik?

5. Jules doesn't like Malik much. Why not? Does her opinion of him match what you read in the first chapter?

6. Based on the second chapter, what kind of kid is Jules?

7. What is your first impression of Mr. Enright?

8. What is the strangest thing to happen in Chapter Three? Why?

9. If you were put in a class like STEM1, would you be excited, nervous, or scared? Why?

10. Does Malik's conversation with Christopher change your opinion of Christopher? Of Malik?

11. Did you come up with any solutions for the leak that the class didn't? How would you have fixed the problem?

12. Did you agree with the class that science is useless? Or do you agree more with Mr. Enright? Why?

13. Can you think of other ways you use STEM every day? What are they?

14. Do you think Dr. Pillai is right to be concerned about the field trip? Would you have stayed behind with her or gone with Mr. Enright?

15. Have you ever seen—or been in—a car that was hydroplaning? Was it scary?

16. Can you think of other ways to fix the neighborhood? What are they?

17. Why did Malik deliberately stand over the fissure?

18. Who is your favorite of the adult experts? Why?

19. Were there other ways the kids could have helped? How?

20. What should Randall have done differently once the flood hit the house?

21. Could the class have done anything differently once the water came rushing toward the house? If so, what?

22. Why is Mr. Enright in the type of boat he has, instead of the kind Malik expected?

23. Is Dr. Pillai right to be so angry at Mr. Enright? Why or why not?

24. Who does Mr. Enright threaten to speak to? Why does Dr. Pillai back off on the idea so quickly?

25. What is your impression of Nancy Enright?

26. What was the most useful thing you learned from the story?

27. Where do you think the class will go next?

28. Which of the careers featured would you be most interested in? Why?

STEM Careers

The STEM kids meet several grown-ups who have STEM-based careers. Here's a little more about each of those jobs, including what you need in order to get one!

ARCHITECTURAL ENGINEER: Architectural engineers use their knowledge of science and technology to design better buildings—ones that improve our quality of life. They do this by making sure all the building's different systems—electrical, mechanical, lighting, acoustics, structural, etc.—work together smoothly. In order to be an architectural engineer, you'll need a bachelor's degree in architectural engineering, preferably from a school approved by the Accreditation Board for Engineering and Technology, or ABET. At last count there were less than 20 ABET-accredited architectural engineering programs in the United States. Depending on what you plan to do with your degree, you may also need to be licensed as a professional engineer, which requires passing two exams from the National Council of Examiners for Engineering and Surveying. The second exam can only be taken after you've had four years of work experience.

ASTRONAUT: (Okay, technically Bud is no longer an astronaut, nor is he human, but he's old enough to be a grown-up, so it still counts!) Astronauts can be divided into two categories: pilots and mission specialists. Pilots are the ones who command and pilot the space shuttles and space stations and are responsible for controlling and operating those vehicles and habitats. To become a pilot astronaut, you need to have a bachelor's degree in engineering, biological science, physical science, or mathematics; to have at least a thousand hours of piloting time in a jet aircraft; and to pass a NASA physical exam. Many pilots have advanced degrees and experience as a test flight pilot as well. Mission specialists handle crew activities, systems, experiments, and payload operations. They are also the ones who perform space walks. Mission specialists need the same sort of bachelor's degree as pilots, but instead of jet piloting experience, they need at least three years of professional experience in their area. Many mission specialists also have advanced degrees. They also need to pass the NASA physical exam.

CIVIL ENGINEER: Civil engineers plan, design, and oversee construction and maintenance of building structures and facilities, such as roads, railways, airports, bridges, dams, power plants, and sewage systems. Like architectural engineers, civil engineers need a bachelor's degree, although theirs should be in civil engineering. Every state requires civil engineers to be licensed, which means not only earning a degree but passing an exam and having at least four years of work experience. The U.S. Bureau of Labor Statistics predicts that employment opportunities for civil engineers will increase by 20% between 2012 and 2022 because as the population grows, cities need to expand, which means more roads, bridges, and buildings.

ECOLOGIST: An ecologist studies nature and the organisms within nature—including man—and how they interact. Most ecologists start out as lab technicians, research assistants, or fieldwork assistants. Many move on to acquire the same degrees as environmental engineers or hydrologists. Ecologists usually teach, conduct research, or serve as consultants and advisors to various agencies and organizations. To become an ecologist, you need a bachelor's degree in ecology. If you want to advance, however, you'll want to earn a master's degree or even a doctorate (Ph.D).

GEOLOGIST: Geologists study earth processes such as earthquakes, landslides, floods, and volcanic eruptions in order to survey areas and draw up safe building plans. Geologists also look into oil, natural gas, and water and methods to extract these. Most geologists work for engineering or environmental consulting firms; oil, gas, or mining companies; science centers and museums; or government agencies. Geologists usually split their time between working in an office and working out in the field collecting data and samples. To be a geologist, you'll need a bachelor's degree in geology or a closely related field like environmental science. Most geologists also have a master's degree in geology, environmental science, or environmental engineering. Some also go on to get a doctorate (Ph.D.) in one of those fields.

HYDROLOGIST: Hydrologists study the physical properties of bodies of water, both in the field and in the lab, to analyze the impact of pollution, erosion, drought, and other problems. Hydrologists spend a lot of time in the field collecting data, so don't go into this field unless you like to travel! To become a hydrologist, you need a master's degree in geoscience, environmental science, or engineering with a concentration in hydrology or water sciences. Most states also require a license, which requires that you take an exam only when you have both the necessary degree and the minimum level of experience. Most hydrologists start out as research assistants, lab technicians, or field exploration assistants. In 2012 there were over 7,000 working hydrologists! Most of them work for either government agencies or consulting firms.

HYDROMETEOROLOGIST: Hydrometeorologists study the interaction between the atmosphere and the land, and the impact that interaction has on human and environmental well-being. Most hydrometeoroligists work for weather forecast centers or government agencies, and they often work in an office—except during floods, when they may be called on to work long hours in the field. Hydrometeorologists are often lumped into the larger category of Atmospheric and Space Scientists, of which more than 10,000 are employed around the United States! A hydrometeorologist needs a bachelor's degree in atmospheric sciences or meteorology, although at some schools the closest degree is atmospheric chemistry and climatology or atmospheric physics and dynamics. Many also get advanced degrees in hydrology, environmental science, or meteorology.

STEM Tools

The kids in STEM class get to hear about, see, and even play with some cool gadgets. Here's a list:

DIGITAL PROJECTORS: These are what create the image of the fake wall hiding the elevator down to the STEM classroom. Digital projectors can provide a movie-quality image against any flat surface, and some people use them instead of conventional televisions.

JUMPER WIRE: This is what Mr. Enright used to bypass the emergency exit's alarm. They're just wires that can clip onto any other wire, screw, or other contact point. Mr. Enright's had some sort of box on it—most likely a basic voltage detector so he'd know if the power went out completely.

AUTO-DRIVING: The STEM bus can drive itself thanks to what's called auto-driving or self-driving. This is a type of automation that lets your car drive to and from destinations without the need for a human driver, using radar to detect other vehicles, lanes, speed limits, stop signs, stoplights, and so on.

WATER FILTRATION SYSTEM: This is a collection of filters you can put rainwater through as you collect it, making water that's cleaner and safer to drink.

PORTABLE CHAIR: Although they don't actually make anything like the collapsible chair Nancy Enright has—yet—you can buy chairs that fold up into something small enough for you to carry around easily. You can even get a folding stool that turns into an odd cane when it's collapsed.

Additional Resources

Flood and Flash Flood Preparedness: The Disaster Center
www.disastercenter.com/guide/flood.html

Floods: Ready.gov
www.ready.gov/floods

Flood Safety: The American Red Cross
www.redcross.org/prepare/disaster/flood

Flash Flooding: The Weather Channel
www.weather.com/safety/floods/news/flash-flooding-vehicle-danger-20140717

Careers in Science: Science Buddies
www.sciencebuddies.org/science-engineering-careers

STEM Disciplines: O-net
www.onetonline.org/find/stem/?t=0&g=Go

STEM: Exploring Science, Technology, Engineering, and Math Careers
www.careerplanning.about.com/od/exploringoccupations/fl/Exploring-STEM-Careers.htm?

Join the
S.T.E.M. Squad Club!

Christopher Wong

Julie Robbins

Malik Jamar

Tracey DeGuerra

Ilyana Desoff

"Meet" the S.T.E.M. Squad and be the first kid in your neighborhood to get your STEM Squad credentials! Joining the club is easy, and once you're a member, you'll get access to:

- Your very own Squad Card and STEM Membership Certificate
- Great resources for Teachers and Students
- Lots of fun math games, science experiments, mazes, puzzles, coloring pages, and more

CERTIFICATE

This is to certify that

_____

is an official member
in good standing of the

S.T.E.M.
SQUAD

and is entitled to all rights and privileges
granted this _____ day of_____

S.T.E.M.
SQUAD

Using your brain has
never been so much fun!

Just visit:
barronsbooks.com/stemsquad/